CODENAME **QUICKSILVER**

Burning Sky

Look out for the other
CODENAME **QUICKSILVER** books

CODENAME
QUICKSILVER

Burning Sky

Allan Jones

Orion
Children's Books

With special thanks to Rob Rudderham

First published in Great Britain in 2012
by Orion Children's Books
a division of the Orion Publishing Group Ltd
Orion House
5 Upper St Martin's Lane
London WC2H 9EA
An Hachette UK company

1 3 5 7 9 10 8 6 4 2

A catalogue record for this book is available from the British Library.

ISBN 978 1 4440 0547 9

Printed in Great Britain by Clays Ltd, St Ives plc

For Phil Jackson

CHAPTER **ONE**

NEW YORK. 21:30 LOCAL TIME.

Zak Archer twisted on the broad leather seat of the Lincoln MKZ and gave a final wave to the cheering crowds as the limousine slid away from the concert hall and nosed smoothly into the traffic of West 57th Street in New York.

He watched the lights of Carnegie Hall disappear into the distance. It was late evening, but the bright lights of the big city shone all around them and the noise of the traffic was loud and constant. New York never slept, and Zak felt as though the spirit of the city had got right inside him. He was wide awake and wired as they glided between the tall buildings. So far Operation Mozart was right on target.

The autograph-hunting crowd at the stage door hadn't noticed that the boy handing out signed CDs through the open window of the limo was not the same one who had wowed them at the concert grand piano only fifteen minutes earlier. The switch had gone perfectly.

Zak grinned as he settled back into the plush leather and loosened his bowtie. A huge bunch of red roses lay at his side, the cellophane wrap crackling. A few remaining CDs were scattered on the seat. He picked one of them up.

The front of the booklet showed a boy of about fourteen, dressed very formally in white tie and tailcoat, with a slightly dreamy, faraway look in the brown eyes that gazed out from behind black-rimmed glasses.

Zak read the fancy lettering. *Alexi Roman Plays Selections from the Classics.* He could see his own reflection in the background of the CD cover. He smiled again and pushed up the black-rimmed glasses that had slid down his own nose.

They were clear glass. Zak had perfect vision. The spectacles were just part of the disguise. Along with the nerdy hair-do and the uncomfortable tuxedo he was wearing. Jeans and a sloppy T-shirt were more Zak's style.

Zak stared at his ghostly reflection alongside Alexi's picture.

"Weird," he said, not for the first time. He still couldn't get over how alike they looked. Zak Archer and Alexi Roman – with just a bad haircut and glasses to help with the illusion, Zak was the boy genius's identical twin!

Which was exactly why Zak had been called in to play the lead role in Project 17's operation.

The limousine came to a sudden juddering halt. Zak peered through the glass screen that separated him from the driver, and out through the windscreen. A bunch of over-excited people were running across the road, disrupting the traffic, laughing and yelling.

The intercom crackled. "Sorry, Mr Roman," came the chauffeur's voice. "It looks like someone's been celebrating a bit too heartily."

"No problem," Zak replied, impersonating Alexi's slightly posh voice. Colonel Hunter had warned him to speak as little as possible, but Zak liked showing off how well he could imitate Alexi's way of talking.

The drunken group wandered off and the traffic started moving again. A couple of turns and a few long straight streets later they approached the tall oblong of golden lights that formed the front of the Waites Hotel.

The chauffeur spun the wheel and the limousine swung off the main street and cruised towards the sloping road that would take them to the private car park under the hotel.

Zak took his Project 17 issue smartphone out of his pocket. It was a slim silvery oval, cutting-edge touch-screen tech, known among the agents as a Mob. He was about to tap out *arrived Waites safely* when he was blinded by a ferocious blast of red light. It was as if the sun had exploded in his face. Almost instantaneously there came a huge erupting roar and a flash of heat and force. It lifted the limousine off the road and sent it spinning end over end through the flaming air.

20 HOURS EARLIER, THE SAME DAY.
UK TIME 06:30.
Dateline: Fortress.

It was only the lack of windows that suggested there was anything strange about the room, but in fact there was one thing in particular that made this room very unusual indeed. It was thirty metres under the ground, at the heart of the sprawling subterranean complex known as Fortress – headquarters of the specialist branch of British Intelligence called Project 17.

Great heavy steel girders spanned the ceiling. Halogen lights bathed the white walls and lit up the rows of tables and chairs that faced a huge plasma screen, which was flickering.

The steel girders supported the weight of five metres of reinforced concrete. Another twenty-five metres above the room, the streets of London teemed with life – and only a handful of the seven and a half million people who lived and worked in the city had the slightest inkling of the things that went on far, far below their bustling feet.

Colonel Hunter stood to one side of the plasma screen. Called 'Control' by his agents, he ran the whole of Project 17. He was tall and gaunt with grey hair, a ramrod-straight back and piercing grey eyes that looked as if they could drill through sheet steel. Facing him from behind the desks were Zak and a group of his fellow agents.

They were being briefed on a new mission.

Operation Mozart.

Zak was still a bit bleary-eyed – he'd been wrenched from a deep sleep by an agent named Switchblade, who had grabbed him by the shoulders and yelled in his ear. "Rise and shine, Silver! Control wants us in the briefing room. Right now." Switch was a big, blond, blue-eyed boy a couple of years older than Zak. A good person to have with you in a tight fix, as Zak had already learned.

Zak had scrambled out of bed and thrown on some clothes. His bedside clock showed 06:12. But these early rises were just one small part of the craziness that came from being on Colonel Hunter's team. And a new mission would mean a welcome diversion from Project 17's schoolroom. Only agents with missions were allowed to skip lessons.

When he had joined Project 17, Zak had been given the codename Quicksilver, but most of the others just called him Silver. Birth names were never used. He had no idea of Switchblade's real name – nor the real identities or backgrounds of any of the other young agents who sat around him in the briefing room. You didn't ask. When someone joined Project 17, a door was closed on their previous life and family. Closed and locked.

At the time, Zak hadn't even known he had a family to lock out. As far as he'd been aware, he'd been orphaned as a baby; and he'd assumed the rest of his life could be found in his Social Services file. There were some foster parents that hadn't worked out, followed by four years in a children's home. The only part of his life that he felt belonged entirely to him was his friendship with his pal Dodge.

Zak had first encountered Dodge on Waterloo Bridge, two or three years ago. The man was obviously homeless, and Zak had taken pity on him – it was winter and he'd looked cold and hungry. Zak had offered him half a sandwich. They had started chatting, and Zak had been surprised at how well-spoken the man was. He kept quoting from poems and stuff like that, which was odd and intriguing. But what Zak had liked straight away about Dodge was the fact that he listened to what Zak had to say. In Zak's experience, that was pretty unusual in an adult.

They'd quickly become friends. Dodge was the only person Zak had told about Project 17. He knew strictly speaking that he shouldn't have told *anyone* – but Dodge had sworn never to repeat anything Zak told him. And Zak trusted Dodge without reservation.

Everything had changed for Zak shortly after joining Project 17. He'd learned that his mother had been an MI5 field agent and that she and his father had been killed in suspicious circumstances three months after he'd been born, while they were on a mission in Canada. And if that wasn't enough to fry his brain, he'd also been told he was the subject of a top-secret MI5 file, opened at the time of his birth.

He had the feeling there were a lot more secrets to be unearthed – especially the truth behind the mysterious MI5 agent with the codename Slingshot. Colonel Hunter had said that Slingshot was not his mother – but Zak wasn't so sure, and one day he'd vowed he'd get to the bottom of the mystery.

"Watch this webcam video," Hunter told them. "I'll explain what it means afterwards."

He pressed a remote control and the flickering on the plasma screen resolved itself into an alarming picture. A man's face filled the screen, sweaty and panicking, hugely enlarged, so that every bead of moisture stood out clearly on his forehead and upper lip. As far as Zak could make out, the background was an ordinary, featureless room.

"Peter," the man gasped. "I'm so sorry . . . they forced me . . . I had to do what they said . . . I had no choice." His eyes darted to the side as though he had heard something sinister. He leaned closer, his fear plainly showing. "I know we haven't seen one another for a long time, but you're the one person I can trust with this. And I know you can do what needs to be done." Again the anxious eyes flickered to one side. "There's going to be a terrorist attack – you have to prevent it."

Zak thought he heard a distant bang, like a door being kicked open.

"The details are in the post to you – but don't try to open it without the key." The man's head snapped around and he got up suddenly so that a filthy and torn shirt filled the screen. His voice was quieter now that he was further from the microphone, but his words were perfectly clear. "Be careful, Peter. You'll destroy it if you try to get in without the key."

A different voice shouted something in the background.

The man bent forwards and his face came back into view. "Protect the boy, Peter . . . you must protect him . . . he's the only one who. . ." The man's voice cut short with a cry. The image swung and tipped over. The screen went blank.

There were a few moments of silence in the briefing room.

Zak was the first to speak. "What was that all about? Who was he?"

"The man's name is Stephen Avon," Colonel Hunter replied.

"The missing electronics genius?" exclaimed Wildcat, an ash-blonde Goth girl agent. She narrowed her sooty black eyes. "Wow – I'd hardly have recognized him. He looks a total wreck and he's lost a lot of weight since his picture was in the news."

Colonel Hunter pressed the remote and a slideshow of newspaper front pages rolled across the screen. The headlines were all variations on *TOP BOFFIN MISSING* or *ELECTRONICS EXPERT WITH MI5 CONNECTIONS DISAPPEARS*.

The static images changed to a television news report. A well-groomed female newsreader was speaking. There was a photo of a smiling and well-fed Stephen Avon on screen at her back.

"Speculation is growing that Dr Stephen Avon, who went missing from his Berkshire home five days ago, may have been in the pay of a foreign power. Fears have risen about Dr Avon's loyalties since it was revealed by MI5 sources that the laboratory where he worked, and where he kept all the files relevant to his experiments in the field of electro-magnetics, was destroyed in a fire on the night of his disappearance."

Colonel Hunter muted the sound. The newsreader's larger-than-life mouth continued to open and close silently at his side.

"Dr Avon has been missing for five months now," said the Colonel. "An extensive international investigation into his whereabouts is still underway, but there have been no new developments for some time." He frowned. "There are three possible explanations for what may have happened to him. One: he defected and took all his research with him. Two: he was abducted. And three: he had some kind of mental breakdown. I think this video makes it quite clear that it was option two."

"When did you get the video, Control?" asked Jackhammer, a hefty square-jawed boy with slick brown hair.

"It arrived just after midnight," said Colonel Hunter.

A small, round-faced boy with big eyes and a deep fringe spoke. "It didn't come through me, Control," he said. "I'd have got an alert."

"I received it on my home laptop, Bug," said the Colonel.

Bug was Project 17's slightly odd über-nerd. All things electronic went through him as he sat alone in his little office with its multiple plasma screens and cutting-edge computer technology.

"He sent it to you personally, Control?" asked Wildcat. "Why would he do that?"

The Colonel's sharp eyes scanned the faces in front of him. "I shared a room with Dr Avon at university many years ago," he said. "We were close friends once, although our careers sent us in different directions once we left university." His eyes glittered. "I knew of his work, of course," he continued. "But when the news broke of his disappearance, I hadn't seen him for fifteen years or more."

Something clicked in Zak's mind. Colonel Hunter's first name must be Peter – that was the name Dr Avon had used. Peter Hunter. It was quite strange to learn that the Colonel even *had* a first name.

"Send the video through to my office, Control," said Bug. "It'll take me five minutes to work out where it came from."

Colonel Hunter gave Bug the ghost of a smile. "I already know, Bug," he said. "I did a trace. It was sent from an internet cafe in Palmetto Bay, Miami."

"So Dr Avon was in America all the time?" said Wildcat. "How weird is that?"

"I made contact with the FBI as soon as I saw the video," Colonel Hunter said. "They didn't know he was there. FBI Special Agents were sent to the address. The room had been hired for the day by a man going by the name of Spencer Arnold. He paid in cash. No luggage. The motel room was empty and there were signs of a disturbance, including the fact that the motel room's internet computer was broken."

"For Spencer Arnold, read Stephen Avon," said Wildcat.

"Who was he scared of, Control? Who was after him?"

"Whoever it was, I think they got him," said Jackhammer under his breath.

Even though it had been a major scandal, Zak only vaguely remembered the news about Dr Avon disappearing. Back then, that kind of thing wouldn't have interested him. Now he was intrigued.

"What kind of work was Dr Avon doing when he went missing?" Zak asked.

"He was working for a research branch of the Ministry of Defence," the Colonel replied. "He was brilliant at university. Streets ahead of everyone else." The Colonel's face grew even graver. "Shortly before his disappearance, I heard that he was involved in pioneering research on electro-magnetic pulses. Pioneering work. He was close to a major breakthrough, I believe."

Zak had never even heard of electro-magnetic pulses.

"EMPs?" said a small, slender girl behind him. "They're supposed to be able to knock out everything electronic within the pulse zone – but I thought it was only theoretical." Zak turned to look at her. Her codename was Moonbeam. She had huge green eyes and long flaming red hair that framed her pale, freckled face. Zak had only met her a couple of times. She'd been away on some special training course for several months.

"Did Dr Avon work out how to use an EMP as a weapon, Control?" she asked. "Is that what this is all about?"

"He was certainly researching the military capabilities of the EMP," growled Colonel Hunter.

"What would an EMP weapon do?" asked Zak.

Switchblade turned to him. "If an electro-magnetic pulse was triggered, everything electrical in its path would be fried," he said. "Everything! Every computer, every electrical circuit, all hospital equipment, electronic files and data – the power grid – it would all be gone. Finished. Finito!"

"If an EMP were set off over London it would cause total chaos," added Moonbeam. "The banks wouldn't be able to function, which would mean there would be no money available for *anything*. Any aeroplanes in the sky would be brought down. Mobile phones would be dead. Traffic lights would all be down. Trains wouldn't run. Electric lighting would be non-existent. The whole city would be a criminal free-for-all, and there would be nothing the Government or the police could do about it."

Zak was still trying to take in the enormity of this when Colonel Hunter began to speak. "It's clear now that Stephen Avon was kidnapped, either by a rogue foreign government, or by a terrorist organization. The fact that Dr Avon tried to warn us of a terrorist attack only confirms this." He looked at Moonbeam. "Clearly, he managed to escape from wherever he was being kept, but as you saw from the video, his captors caught up with him again."

Zak could see how that made sense. Dr Avon had obviously been terrified in the video. Someone had crashed in on him right in the middle of the webcam recording.

"Dr Avon referred to a boy," said Switchblade. "Do you know who he was talking about, Control?"

"Yes, I do," said Colonel Hunter. He turned back to the screen and clicked the remote.

A photo came up on screen. It was of a boy. Zak guessed he was probably about fourteen – Zak's own age. He was sitting on a stool facing a grand piano. He had short black hair that didn't look as if it had ever been anywhere near a decent hairdresser or any styling gel. He was wearing horrible black-rimmed glasses and an old-fashioned polo neck jumper. He had a wistful, faraway look in his brown eyes, as though he was off in his own little world.

Zak was slightly puzzled by a number of sharply indrawn breaths around him. Jackhammer gave a stifled snort of laughter and Switch murmured a soft "*Wow – talk about snap!*"

"This is Alexi Roman," said Hunter. "Dr Avon was with him about an hour before he made contact with me. I believe this must be the boy Stephen Avon was referring to in his message."

"And if Dr Avon said you needed to protect him, he must be in some kind of danger?" said Switchblade, glancing curiously at Zak from the corner of his eye. "Something to do with the terrorist attack?"

Why was everyone being so weird suddenly?

"I think that's a reasonable expectation," said the Colonel. "Fortunately, we're in the perfect position to keep Alexi Roman from harm." His eyes fixed on Zak. "We can supply a very convincing substitute."

The faces of all the other agents also turned to Zak.

"What?" asked Zak, starting to feel uncomfortable. "What's everyone looking at me for?"

Wildcat stared at him. "You're kidding?" she said. "Don't you see it?" She gestured towards the screen. "You're the spitting image of him, Silver!"

Zak stared at the enlarged photo of the geeky boy then back at Wildcat, aghast.

"I am not!" he gasped.

Switch poked him in the ribs. "Trust me, some black hair dye, a bad haircut and some truly horrible glasses and you're *him*!"

"And you're booked on a flight to New York this afternoon, Quicksilver," said Colonel Hunter. "This time tomorrow, you're going to *be* Alexi Roman."

CHAPTER **TWO**

"It could be worse," said Wildcat with a barely suppressed grin.

She and Switchblade were standing behind Zak as he sat in front of a large brightly lit mirror, staring unhappily at his new reflection.

They were in a set of rooms in Fortress called Chameleon 04. This was where agents were given disguises if they needed to blend into the background for a specific mission. Zak hadn't been here before, and he wasn't enjoying his first visit very much.

It could be worse?

"It could?" Zak asked Wildcat, gazing gloomily up at her in the mirror. His hair had been dyed black and restyled. Well, *restyled* was hardly the word in Zak's opinion – *unstyled* was more like it. Alexi Roman had anti-style hair – and now Zak did too. He hated the glasses – they felt heavy and weird, and they looked ridiculous. "How could it possibly be worse?"

"Alexi could have had rampant acne and wonky teeth," Switch suggested.

"Spots and dental braces I could live with," Zak said. "It's the hair that's doing my head in. Look at it!" Usually, Zak's brown hair stood up in a spiky gelled spray, now it was dyed black and cut too short and flattened down with a sharp parting along one side. It made him look like a mental case. Worse – it made him look like the kind of kid who loved maths exams.

Wildcat laughed. "I had no idea you were so vain, Silver," she said.

Zak glowered at her.

"You know what," Switch said thoughtfully. "I think it really suits you."

"That's it!" Zak yelled, getting up. "I quit! Where's Control, I'm handing in my resignation right now!"

"That's a pity, I had high hopes for you, Quicksilver." Zak spun towards the door. He hadn't heard Colonel

Hunter enter. The Colonel had an uncanny trick of suddenly appearing in rooms like that. Silently, like a tiger on the prowl.

"Uh . . . I was . . . only . . ." Zak stammered, his face burning red.

"Bug has downloaded all the information you'll need about Alexi Roman onto your Mob," the Colonel said, ignoring Zak's embarrassment. "You'll have the details of his American tour, and the full Legend." Legend was Project 17 code for a person's background details. "You can go through it on the aeroplane. Bug has also downloaded a radio interview Alexi Roman did a few weeks ago. Listen to the way he expresses himself – try and learn to speak like him."

"I'm not sure I can do an American accent," Zak admitted.

"He isn't American, he's English," said the Colonel. "Read the file. Switchblade – you and Moonbeam will be flying with Quicksilver to New York."

Zak glanced at Wildcat, wondering why she hadn't been chosen this time.

"Moonbeam has the perfect training for this particular mission," the Colonel added, almost as if he'd read Zak's mind. Seeing Zak's look, Wildcat winked and smiled.

"The full details will be on your Mobs by the time you

get to Heathrow Airport," Colonel Hunter finished. He looked appraisingly at Zak for a few moments. Zak got the definite impression that he was trying not to smile. "Excellent work, Molly," he said to the woman who had been in charge of Zak's makeover. "Some of your best."

"Thank you, Control," said the woman.

"Okay," said the Colonel, turning on his heel and marching towards the door. "Be smart, be safe – and keep me updated. Your flight leaves in three hours."

The Boeing 747-400 jet airliner departed from Heathrow Airport at 15:05 local time. Zak and Moonbeam had adjoining seats; Switchblade was just across the aisle. Within an hour the airliner was at a height of 10,660 metres above the Atlantic, cruising at 920 kph with the sun reflecting like white fire off its wings.

Zak used the time to check his Mob for the info Bug had downloaded for him. There was a lot to take in.

Classical piano prodigy Alexi Roman was brought up by his grandmother in the Surrey town of Guildford, following the tragic death of his parents in a boating accident when he was an infant.

Zak paused. Alexi Roman had lost his parents? That was something they had in common. He carried on reading.

An only child, Alexi revealed his extraordinary talent for the piano as early as four years old. He was a neighbour of Dr Steven Avon, the renowned electronics expert, whose extraordinary disappearance made headline news a few months ago. The extent of Alexi's talent was recognized early on by Dr Avon, who was also an accomplished amateur pianist. In fact, Dr Avon was Alexi's first piano tutor, and continued to give the budding genius piano lessons until he was ten, when Dr Avon moved away to pursue his career in another part of the country.

Zak paused again in his reading. He had wondered what the link could be between Dr Avon and Alexi Roman. Now he knew – but even that information didn't answer all of the questions that were still buzzing in his brain. He scrolled down the small bright screen of the Mob.

By the time he was eight, Alexi had begun to make public appearances, receiving rave reviews from critics, and showing the promise of a great career ahead of him, playing the classics at concert halls all over the world.

At the age of twelve, his first album was released, accompanied by YouTube videos and a significant internet publicity campaign. The album quickly climbed to the Number 1 spot in the classical music charts, and stayed there for seven weeks.

Although shy and reserved in public, Alexi Roman has become very popular with his fans and was invited to tour the United States shortly after his fourteenth birthday. To prepare for his tour, he stayed at the beachside mansion of classical music enthusiast and philanthropist Marcus Goodman, a well-known and respected resident of Palmetto Bay in Miami, Florida.

Alexi's first performance will be at Carnegie Hall in New York, where he will play many popular pieces including Beethoven's much loved Sonata No. 28 . . .

Zak didn't bother to read the rest of the article. Instead he flicked the touch-screen of his Mob and brought up a Project 17 file.

Alexi Roman Legend Update.

The FBI has managed to keep some facts from the international news media.

On a timeline that places it only an hour before he made webcam contact from the Blue Palm Motel, Stephen Avon was at Marcus Goodman's beach house in Palmetto Bay, Miami. Undetected by staff or residents, he managed to gain access to the suite of rooms being used by Alexi Roman. The two spoke briefly before Stephen Avon left the beach house again. His whereabouts are currently unknown despite a concentrated covert search operation by the FBI in the Palmetto Bay region.

Roman had been interviewed on the radio the day before Avon appeared. We can safely assume that Avon learned of Roman's whereabouts by listening to this interview. This meant he had access to a radio, but was this before he escaped or afterwards?

According to Alexi Roman, Stephen Avon seemed nervous and on edge throughout their brief meeting, but he insists they spoke only of the forthcoming American tour and of music in general. Despite Alexi asking, Avon did not explain where he had been, nor what had happened to him in the last five months. He wished Roman good luck and then left.

Our belief is that Avon had escaped his long-term captors and was on the run. The fact that he made first contact with Alexi Roman is highly significant. There are two explanations for this. 1: he did not trust the authorities. 2: he was being held close to where Roman was staying and only had time to make contact with him.

Either way, it is vital that we learn every detail of what went on between Stephen Avon and Alexi Roman. We are in no doubt that Avon passed some vital piece of information to Roman without the boy realizing its importance.

The interrupted video link to Control suggests that Avon was recaptured. We must assume his captors were close on his trail and that they may already know of the meeting between him and Roman. If this is the case, Roman may be in danger from them. Avon himself seemed to believe this to be true.

We need to ensure Alexi Roman's security

until he can be fully debriefed. Operation Mozart
will involve Quicksilver impersonating Roman
after his first concert in New York and leading
any potential threat away, while Switchblade
takes Roman in disguise to John F Kennedy
Airport for a flight to London Heathrow.

To ensure that Roman is safe in Fortress
before news leaks, Quicksilver and Moonbeam
will fly to Miami where Roman is due to appear
at the Gusman Concert Hall. From there, the
cancellation of the tour will be announced and
Moonbeam and Quicksilver will return to Fortress.

Zak looked up from his Mob and glanced at Moonbeam,
who was sitting next to him and scrolling on her own Mob.

"Are you reading Control's Legend update?" he asked
her.

She nodded. "Control's right," she said. "Dr Avon must
have told Alexi something vital – something to do with
the terrorist attack he warned about in the video."

Zak nodded. "Something that he thought Alexi Roman
would understand," he said. "Except, so far as we know,
Alexi didn't understand it at all."

"Control will figure it out when he debriefs Alexi,"
Moonbeam said. "Speaking of Control." She pulled

something from the pocket of her jeans. "He asked me to give you this."

Zak took it. It was small, not much bigger than a lipstick. It looked like a mouth spray.

"If something goes wrong, you can use this to get yourself out of a bad situation," she told him.

He held it dubiously between finger and thumb. "And how will having minty-fresh breath get me out of trouble?" he asked.

Moonbeam smiled. "It's not a mouth spray," she said. "It's called a Kiss. Take the top off."

Zak did as she suggested. "And. . .?" he asked, seeing nothing remarkable.

"It has a compressed-air jet-injection system built in," Moonbeam explained. "Hold it against someone's bare skin and press the end – it'll blast a powerful sleeping drug right through the epidermis. They'll go out like a light. Three seconds flat."

"Cool," murmured Zak, replacing the lid and slipping the device into his pocket. "Way cool!"

Zak spent the rest of the seven-hour flight to New York watching downloaded YouTube videos of Alexi Roman in action at the piano, and listening to interviews. His voice was slightly higher than Zak's, rather nasal and a bit more posh. Zak tried speaking aloud along to the interviews that were being piped into his ear, taking one earphone out so he could hear himself properly. Stewards walking past gave him some odd looks.

Zak didn't mind the looks – he had other things to think about. He was flying to America for the first time in his life – and he was going there on a secret mission to impersonate a complete stranger. If his mission failed, there was the threat of a terrorist attack that could wipe out a whole city's worth of electrical data and information.

Everyone's relying on me. Can I really do this?

He looked up, needing to distract himself from his worries. Moonbeam was busy with an aviation manual, he noticed.

"Excuse me, Moon," he asked, doing his best to sound like Alexi. "Why are you reading that?"

"Homework," Moonbeam said. She nodded at him. "That's good, Zak. You're getting it."

"What if people want autographs?" Zak asked.

"Control has arranged for a pile of pre-signed CDs to be available," said Moonbeam. "You just smile and hand them out. Easy." She looked at him. "Have you ever been to New York before?"

Zak shook his head. "Never."

"It's a great place," she said. "You'll really like it. It's a total blast!"

CHAPTER **THREE**

The Graves House was a great white stone mansion on the corner of 82nd Street and Lexington Avenue. The luxurious apartment where Alexi Roman was staying was on the top floor, high above the busy New York streets.

The three Project 17 agents were met by FBI Special Agent Dean Carter and by the people who were travelling with Alexi.

Special Agent Carter wore a dark suit. He had blond hair and pale, unreadable eyes, although it was the slow Southern drawl that Zak found most fascinating. He'd heard the accent on TV, but he'd never actually met anyone who really spoke like that.

Special Agent Carter introduced everyone. There was a man called Gregory Isaacs who helped Alexi with his daily piano practice. Next was a tutor called Mr Bryce who made sure Alexi kept up with his schoolwork while he was on the road. There were a couple of young female PAs who flitted about trying to look important, and there was Alexi's manager, Lindsey Stark, a tall, formidable-looking woman who clearly thought this whole exercise was a waste of time.

"As if Dr Avon would harm the boy," she said, looking Zak up and down with a caustic eye. "And you're supposed to look like Alexi, are you, young man?" she said. She snorted. "There's a slight resemblance, I suppose."

"The glasses help," said Zak, taking them out of his pocket and putting them on.

"Well, I suppose you have to do what you came here to do." She sniffed. "I don't know why. This is a ridiculous overreaction. It's perfectly obvious that Alexi knows nothing about what Dr Avon has been doing for the last few months. And Stephen Avon is in Florida, the poor man – evidently sick in his mind." She glared at Special Agent Carter. "You should be putting your efforts into finding the poor chap, rather than disrupting Alexi on the first night of the most important tour of his life." She wagged a finger. "If Alexi is put off his playing by your foolishness, I'll be speaking to the British Ambassador, you can count on that."

Special Agent Carter nodded and said "Yes, ma'am," every now and then. "I think it would be good for Alexi and Agent Quicksilver to spend a little time together, ma'am," he said once the manager had run out of steam. "Just to get to know one another."

"Very well," she replied. "He's practising in the Blue Room."

"Meanwhile, we'd like to fill you in on exactly what we have planned," said Switchblade.

"Ruining Alexi's career, that's what you have planned," complained the manager. "Cancelling the tour after one performance! He's due to perform in Miami, Memphis, Dallas, Phoenix and Los Angeles. Who will be responsible for informing the venues that he won't be appearing? Who will be responsible for repaying the ticket monies?"

"The tour isn't being cancelled," Moonbeam said coaxingly. "Only postponed. As soon as we know all the facts, and as soon as we know Alexi is safe, the tour can continue. The FBI will handle any problems." She looked at Special Agent Carter. "Won't they?"

"Sure thing, ma'am," said Special Agent Carter.

"He is safe *now*, you foolish child," snapped the manager. "This is all a complete waste of time."

"Where's the Blue Room?" Zak asked, already tired of the manager's grumbling. It was bad enough knowing he was making himself the target for any attack on Alexi, without being told the whole mission was pointless.

He was led away by the piano tutor.

The soft, subdued sound of a piano could be heard behind a tall door.

"Thanks," Zak said, taking the handle. "I'll be fine now."

The tutor nodded and left him to it.

Zak knocked. A familiar voice called out. A voice he'd been listening to very carefully on the flight to New York.

"Come in."

Zak entered a long, elegant room with blue curtains and a blue carpet. A grand piano dominated the middle of the room. Alexi Roman was sitting on the stool. His eyebrows rose and his mouth dropped open as Zak walked across the room.

"Hello," said Zak. "I'm Project 17 Agent Quicksilver, but you can call me Silver. I was. . ."

"Do I really look like that?" Alexi interrupted him.

Zak stopped in his tracks. "Sorry?"

"Do I really look that bad?" Alexi began to laugh. Zak watched him in surprise for a few moments. Alexi was rocking back and forth, shaking with laughter. Zak found himself grinning at the laughing boy.

"Don't you *know* what you look like?" Zak asked him.

"Well, yes, but. . ." Alexi convulsed with laughter again. "I'm a total nerd!"

Zak's forehead creased. "Well, yes . . . you kind of are . . . a bit . . ." he admitted, moving closer. "But it's nothing that can't be improved. You just need some cooler glasses and a seriously urgent visit to a good hairdresser . . . and maybe you could buy your clothes in a shop that has fewer granddads as customers." His grin widened. "Apart from that . . ."

Alexi calmed down, wiping his streaming eyes.

"Silver is a weird name," he said, looking Zak up and down.

"It's my codename," Zak explained.

"You're really a British Secret Service agent?" asked Alexi incredulously. "At your age?"

Zak smiled. "You're really an internationally famous piano genius . . . at *your* age?" he replied.

Alexi gazed thoughtfully at him for a moment. "That's

because I'm gifted ... apparently," he said, looking slightly awkward. "I'm not really sure what that means – except that I can do something other people mostly can't. You know, playing the piano like I do."

"I've got a gift as well," said Zak.

"Really? What is it?"

"I can run fast." Zak's eyes gleamed as he looked at Alexi. "I mean, *really* fast. Crazy fast. It's because of some weird stuff in my adrenal gland."

"Cool," breathed Alexi.

"I guess so," said Zak.

Zak and Alexi looked at one another for a few moments, as if they were silently bonding over both being a little strange.

"So, is Dr Avon in trouble?" Alexi asked, and there was a catch in his voice now. "I really like him – I don't want bad stuff happening to him."

Zak didn't quite know how to respond. "The people I work with are really good at what they do," he said at last, smiling reassuringly. "If they can't help him, no one can."

Alexi nodded. "That's good to know." He looked at Zak. "Tell me if I've got this right," he said. "The plan is that I play at Carnegie Hall tonight, then we switch over and you get into the car that's meant to take me back to the Waites Hotel. And the bad guys – whoever they might be – they're supposed to follow you while I'm whisked away to the airport by one of your pals."

"That's pretty much the plan," Zak said.

"Who exactly are the bad guys?" Alexi asked. "What do they want?"

"We don't know for sure," said Zak. "But they could be dangerous. That's why we're here." All Project 17 information was given out on a need-to-know basis. Alexi didn't need to know any more than he had already been told: Dr Avon was on the run from some bad people, some dangerous terrorists, and there was a chance that Alexi might get caught up in it because of the meeting in Miami.

"What if someone speaks to you while you're being me?" asked Alexi. "You don't sound like me at all."

Zak put on his impression of Alexi's voice. "Then I'll talk to them like this," he said. "What do you think?"

It was another minute or so before Alexi stopped laughing.

Zak had to admit that this was going way better than he had expected – under the layers of nerd, there was definitely a very cool person trying to get out.

"Do you really think Dr Avon is wrong in the head?" asked Alexi, suddenly becoming serious again. "It was kind of creepy meeting him like that in Florida – but I don't think he was acting crazy. He was talking perfectly normally, except that he wouldn't tell me where he'd been since he disappeared." He shook his head. "I don't get it."

"We don't know what's going on yet," said Zak. "But we're pretty sure he said something important – something to do with a terrorist attack."

"I know," said Alexi. "Special Agent Carter and some other people said the same thing – but he didn't." His voice was insistent. "He really didn't."

Zak quietly slipped his hand into his pocket and activated the record facility on his Mob. If he could get Alexi talking about the meeting with Dr Avon, and record it, he could play it back over and over, and maybe figure out what Dr Avon had secretly been trying to tell him.

"I know this is a total pain," Zak said. "But could you go through everything you can remember that Dr Avon said to you? It's not a big deal if you can't remember it all."

"I remember everything," Alexi said. "I was practising Mozart's Piano Sonata Number 16, and suddenly he was behind me. He came in through the French windows that led onto the beach." Alexi frowned. "He looked bad – as if he hadn't slept. He was wearing a long coat that he kept buttoned up. That was weird in itself, because it was really hot." He paused, as though gathering his thoughts. "He came and sat by me at the piano. I was really shocked but he told me everything was fine. I asked him where he had been all this time – you know, since he was in the news." Zak nodded, watching Alexi intently. "He told me he'd been working somewhere secret and secluded. He said he couldn't tell me about it right now, but that everything would be explained very soon."

"He didn't give you any idea at all where he'd been for the past five months?"

Alexi shook his head. "Like I said, I asked, but he wouldn't say, even though I told him everyone had been worried about him," he said. "He was really great to me when I was first learning to play – and even when he had to go away, he always remembered my birthday and sent me stuff at Christmas." He looked at Zak fiercely. "He isn't mad, and I don't think he could have done anything bad, either. I won't believe that."

"Did he say anything else?" Zak urged him.

"He said he was thrilled to hear about my American tour," Alexi said. "He said he heard about it on the radio."

So, Control had got that right. The trigger that had brought Dr Avon to Alexi was the radio interview.

"He didn't give you any clue at all about where he'd been?" Zak asked again.

Alexi shook his head adamantly. "No! People keep asking me that, but he didn't. He didn't say a word about it." A faint, sad smile appeared on his face. "He said he hadn't been able to practise his playing at all – there was a piano in the place where he was staying, he told me, but he wasn't allowed to play." Alexi frowned. "I thought that was a bit strange. Why would anyone stop him playing?" Alexi ran his fingers over the keys of the piano, playing a brief, lilting melody. "He said he came up with that tune in his head," Alexi said, playing it again. "He played it for me a couple of times – he said it was the first time he'd actually heard it out loud." Alexi stopped playing and stared at Zak. "We talked about music for a little while and then he left. Out through the French windows and across the beach." He sighed. "That was it. I told people about it later – although now I really wish I hadn't, because it freaked everyone out. Then there was the FBI and the British Ambassador and all sorts of other people, asking me the same questions over and over."

"And now I'm doing it," said Zak. "Sorry." He reached into his pocket and turned off the recording.

Alexi shrugged. "I wish he *had* told me something," he

mumbled. "Something to help you find him."

"We'll find him," Zak said, trying to sound convincing. "He'll be fine. No problem."

Alexi looked at him solemnly but said nothing.

There was a knock on the door. It opened a fraction and Moonbeam's face appeared. "I'm to tell you it's time, Alexi," she said. "Silver – you're coming with us in a different car and with a hoodie over your head. We don't want anyone getting wind of the switch in advance." She nodded to the two boys. "Operation Mozart is underway, guys – good luck."

Zak sat alone in a small dressing room backstage at Carnegie Hall. He was wearing a tuxedo, and he felt nerdier than he had ever thought possible. Alexi was onstage – playing his heart out for the packed audience.

Zak was plugged into his Mob, listening to the conversation he'd had with Alexi earlier that evening. He had hoped something would leap out at him – something that no one else had noticed. He had imagined himself making sudden urgent contact with Colonel Hunter.

Hi, Control – I've figured out what Dr Avon said to Alexi.

That would have been sweet.

An award for braininess above and beyond the call of

duty? No, really – you're embarrassing me, Control. Well . . . if you think I deserve it . . .

But he'd listened to Alexi's recorded voice ten or more times now – and there was nothing. Nothing at all.

Piano music was being piped into the dressing room over a loudspeaker system. Zak turned the Mob recording off and listened as the piano piece came to a swirling, crashing crescendo. Zak was no fan of classical music, but he had to admit Alexi could play like a demon.

There was a moment's silence then a burst of applause and cheering erupted from the loudspeaker.

Zak glanced at the time on his Mob. Yes, that was it. The concert was over. The door opened. Switch was there.

"Ready?" he asked.

Zak got up, nodding.

"Don't stop for autographs or a chat," Switch reminded him. "Just walk straight to the car, get in and go. You can hand out these signed albums." Switch handed him a pile of CDs. "Remember. Wave and smile. As soon as you get to the Waites Hotel, text me. You'll make a very brief appearance at the reception, then they'll say you're not feeling well, and you'll be taken to your room. Stay there till you hear from me or Moonbeam. Once you're at the hotel, I'll slip out and take Alexi to John F Kennedy

Airport. Moonbeam will be going to Miami with you, so she can help you if you get into trouble."

"What trouble?" asked Zak. "It's all cool. I know what to do."

The applause seemed to go on for a long, long time. Zak imagined Alexi bowing and waving at the crowds. It must be nice to be cheered at. The most he ever got was Colonel Hunter telling him *well done*.

At last, the clapping and shouting died down. A few minutes later, Alexi came into the room, looking tired but excited, with a huge bunch of red roses in his arms.

"It sounded good," Zak said, seeing a wild feverish light in Alexi's eyes. "Was it good?"

"The audience seemed to think so," breathed Alexi. "I'm wrecked! The Liszt really takes it out of me."

Zak took the roses from him, juggling them with the CDs.

"Good luck," said Alexi, collapsing into an armchair.

"See you in London," Zak replied. He headed along the corridor to the back exit of the concert hall. Next stop, the Waites Hotel for the post-concert reception.

Everything was going exactly to plan.

A crowd was waiting outside the stage door. Zak smiled and waved and handed out a few signed CDs as he made his way to the waiting limousine. He clambered inside, winding down the window to push CDs into the eager hands of Alexi's more persistent fans.

The limo moved off. Zak twisted around and gave a final wave to the cheering crowds as the limousine slid away from the concert hall and nosed smoothly into the traffic of West 57th Street in New York.

CHAPTER **FOUR**

**JOHN F KENNEDY INTERNATIONAL
AIRPORT.
TERMINAL 7. GATE 12.
22:12 LOCAL TIME.**

Switchblade made his way quickly through the departure gate and walked along the ramp that led to the waiting Boeing 777-200. Alexi was at his side, his face shadowed by a hoodie.

Alexi knew something was wrong, but the tall blond-haired boy wouldn't tell him anything. A call had come through while they'd been waiting at the concert hall. Switchblade's face had gone white with shock and suddenly everything had become urgent and deadly serious.

Alexi had changed into casual clothes and Switchblade had raced him along the corridors to a waiting car, yanking his hood over his head and drawing it down to hide his face.

A wild drive to the airport had followed, with Switchblade constantly texting on that weird silvery smartphone of his. And between texts, Switchblade kept staring out through the back windows of the car, as though he was afraid that they were being tailed.

But no matter how often Alexi asked, the agent had told him nothing.

They'd met Special Agent Carter at the airport. He had led them through check-in and passport control faster than Alexi had ever believed possible, bypassing the usual queues and protocols.

Flight 182, direct to London Heathrow, had been called after a few minutes. Switchblade and Special Agent Carter shook hands, their faces grim.

"Good luck, young fella," the FBI Special Agent said briefly to Alexi, before turning and striding away, already talking into his smartphone.

They boarded the aeroplane and found their seats.

A soft chime from Switchblade's strange smartphone announced the arrival of another text.

Alexi looked at him, not bothering to ask a question he knew would not be answered.

As Switchblade read the text, a sudden change came over his face. There was an expression of absolute relief. He leaned his head back and blew out his cheeks. "He's okay," he gasped, looking at Alexi. "I thought for a while . . ." He paused. "He's fine. Jut a few cuts and bruises is all."

Alexi poked him in the ribs. "So, now will you tell me what's going on?" he demanded.

Switchblade looked at him keenly for a few moments before he spoke.

"Quicksilver is okay," he said slowly, bringing his mouth close to Alexi's ear and speaking in little more than a whisper. "But there was an incident . . ."

LENNOX HILL HOSPITAL. MANHATTAN.

Zak was sitting up in a bed in a private room. The journey in the ambulance and the whirlwind of activity around him in the ER room were just a vague blur – but his brain was starting to clear now and he was beginning to remember what had happened.

His head ached and he was hurting in so many places that it felt as though he'd been whacked all over with a cricket bat. A couple of doctors were looking at charts at the foot of his bed, and Moonbeam was talking in a low voice to Special Agent Cooper.

"How's the driver?" Zak asked, wincing as the sound of his own voice made his head pulse with pain.

Moonbeam turned to him with a smile. "Not too bad," she said, gliding around the bed. "Two broken legs and some busted up ribs. A broken wrist and suspected concussion. You look a bit of a mess right now, but they say you'll be okay." She frowned into Zak's face. "How are you doing?"

"Never felt better," Zak said, wincing again as he pulled himself up further on the bunched pillows. "Apart from the all the agony and stuff."

Moon looked closely at his forehead. "You have a cut on your head just above your hairline, but it's been stitched," she said. "Your hair covers it fine. Does it hurt a lot?"

"It depends what you mean by a *lot.*" Zak forced himself to focus on Moonbeam's face. "Someone wanted Alexi dead, didn't they?" he said softly. "That was a bomb that went off in our faces."

Moon stood up and turned to the doctors. "Could we have the room, please?" she asked.

The doctors gave her a surprised look, but Special Agent Cooper walked to the door and opened it, gesturing for them to leave.

Once the doctors were gone, Special Agent Cooper sat on the edge of Zak's bed. "We don't have any forensics yet," he said. "But we think the bomb was detonated by a timer."

"It looks as if the bomb was set in the roof of the tunnel that led to the car park under the hotel," said Moonbeam. "We don't think the bomber could have had eye-contact with the car – we think it was due to blow either as you passed along the tunnel, or once you were in the car park.'

"How much damage did it do?" asked Zak. His brain was clearing now. "Is the hotel still in one piece? Was anyone else hurt?"

"The hotel is fine," said Special Agent Cooper. "The effects of the blast were contained within the parking zone. The roof came in and about fifty cars got totalled – but fortunately, the rest of the hotel is safe. And no one else was injured."

"We stopped," Zak said, remembering the run-up to the explosion. "There were some people messing about in the street." He shuddered as the full reality hit him. "If not for that we would have been right under the bomb."

"It's better to be born lucky than rich," said Moonbeam with a grin. She went to her shoulder bag and drew out a laptop. She sat on the other side of the bed, opened the laptop and began typing.

"Did Alexi and Switch get away safely?" Zak asked.

"It all went to plan," said Special Agent Cooper. He glanced at his watch. "About now they should be over the Atlantic. Well out of harm's way."

Moon turned the laptop towards Zak. Colonel Hunter's face was on-screen.

"I'm glad to see you're all right, Quicksilver," said the Colonel. "You did a good job. Well done."

Well done.

No cheering, then. No riotous applause.

But Colonel Hunter's quiet approval meant more to Zak than a whole concert hall full of people yelling their heads off.

"Thanks, Control," said Zak. "What's next?"

"Our caution has proved well-founded," said the Colonel. "Someone wants Alexi Roman dead, that's certain now. The sooner he arrives at Fortress the better. I need to start debriefing him as quickly as possible. We mustn't forget that there's a terrorist threat at the back of all this. A lot of lives may depend on us finding out the truth. "

"On the webcam link, Dr Avon said that the details of the attack were in the post," said Zak. "Has anything arrived?"

Colonel Hunter shook his head. "There's been nothing so far," he said. "I've got people standing by. The moment anything unusual arrives at my home address, I'll be alerted."

"Do you think Dr Avon is still alive, sir?" asked Special Agent Cooper.

"Until I get news to the contrary, yes," replied the Colonel. "Is there anything new from the FBI crime scene team at the motel?"

Special Agent Cooper shook his head. "Nothing," he said. "Whoever took him did a really clean job, sir."

"If they're prepared to kill Alexi Roman, they obviously don't need to get their hands on whatever information Dr Avon passed to him," said Moonbeam. "They just want to stop him from telling anyone else."

"That's my take on it," said Colonel Hunter. "My belief is that whatever information Stephen Avon passed to Alexi concerns the thing he put in the post – hopefully it's the key to getting it open – whatever it is."

"The FBI are with you all the way on this, sir," said Special Agent Cooper. "Just say the word, and we'll do whatever it takes."

"Right now, I just need you to control the story over there," said the Colonel. "How is it being played in the media?"

"We've managed to give the impression it was a gas mains blow-out," said Special Agent Cooper. "The news media are buying it for now, but we may not be able to contain it for long."

"We just need a few hours," said the Colonel. "Quicksilver? Are you fit enough to continue with the mission?"

Zak sat up straight in bed, ignoring the discomfort. "Yes, Control. Of course."

"The bombers will know you survived," Colonel Hunter said grimly. "They aren't going to give up." His eyes turned away from Zak. "Moonbeam – I need you to initiate Operation Honeybee."

"Got it, Control," said Moonbeam. Zak saw her eyes shining, as though the idea of Operation Honeybee excited her. Zak had not heard of it before. He assumed it was some kind of back-up plan to be set in motion if things got tricky.

And things had definitely got tricky.

BOEING 777-222 FLIGHT 182, JOHN F KENNEDY AIRPORT TO LONDON HEATHROW.

Cruising at 490 knots, 13,000 metres above the North Atlantic. On schedule. Due to arrive London Heathrow Terminal 3 at 10:40 local time.

Alexi stared at Switchblade. "Someone tried to kill me?" he breathed. "Because Dr Avon came and talked to me?"

"We think so," Switchblade replied. "But you're safe now. And you'll stay safe until we get to the bottom of this."

Alexi's eyes widened in alarm. "And if you don't?"

"We will," said Switchblade.

"If they try again, Silver might get killed," Alexi murmured. "Because of me."

"Quicksilver will be fine," Switch said with a reassuring smile. "He can run faster than any bomb." He leaned closer. "He's not doing this just because he looks like you, Alexi. He's fully trained, and he has some special . . ." He paused, choosing the word. ". . . abilities. You'd be amazed."

"Yes, he told me," said Alexi. "The running thing." He blinked at Switchblade through his thick glasses. "So, is he well enough to take the train to Miami?"

The next stop on Alexi's American tour was to be the Gusman Concert Hall in Miami, Florida. He was due to perform there in two nights' time. Zak would go to Miami as Alexi and keep up the illusion until the real Alexi was safe inside Fortress. Then there would be a news bulletin announcing that Alexi Roman had been taken ill, the tour would be postponed, and Zak and Moon would make their way back to London.

That was the idea.

If everything went according to plan.

"He won't be travelling by train," Switchblade told Alexi. "Your manager and the others will be taking the Silver Star from Penn Station tomorrow morning at eleven."

"And Silver? How's he getting there?"

Switchblade smiled. "He'll be flying down there overnight," he said. "The FBI has helped us organize something special for him and Moon." His eyes gleamed. "Something very unusual. We had to sidestep several dozen protocols to get it done." A knowing smile curled the corners of his mouth. "I think Quicksilver is in for quite a surprise."

Moon had been strangely reluctant to give Zak the full details of their flight to Miami. All she told him was that a private plane had been chartered for the two-and-a-half-hour night-time flight.

The doctors at Lennox Hill had given Zak a final check, then he'd dressed in some of Alexi's sadly unfashionable clothes, combed his hair and put on the fake nerdy glasses, before being bundled out of the hospital past yelling reporters and strobing camera-flashes. Alexi Roman's near-catastrophic encounter with the exploding gas mains was big news. As Zak had been helped into a waiting car, Alexi's manager had been live on the TV news, giving an update on the situation and telling people everything was okay and the tour was going ahead as planned. Alexi would be flying to Miami from La Guardia on a private charter, arriving early to give him plenty of time to rest and recover before the next concert.

Zak let out a relieved breath as the car door slammed, shutting out the clamour. He guessed the driver was FBI. Moon joined him in the back of the car a couple of minutes later, and they sped away into the neon-lit New York night.

"Feeling up to the job?" Moon asked as they drove through the streets.

"Of course," Zak replied.

She looked at him, one eyebrow arched.

"I'm okay," he told her. "Really. No problems at all."

"You've just been blown up, Silver," she said. "You must hurt all over. You don't need to fake it with me."

"It's all good," he insisted.

She shrugged. "Be like that then."

"What are you, my social worker all of a sudden?"

Strangely enough, Zak really didn't feel that bad. His head was still rumbling like a distant thunderstorm and he was stiff and uncomfortable, but apart from that he felt fine. The doctors at Project 17 had told him he had an unusual adrenaline imbalance; it was what made him able to run so fast. Perhaps the weird stuff that went on inside him was healing his injuries, or at least masking the pain and the aftershocks.

Either way, he was glad of it. He wanted to be a hundred per cent when the next attempt on Alexi's life hit.

It was a long drive and Zak was content just to sit back and watch the lights and the traffic and the milling people as they flicked past. Every now and then a loud sound, a revving engine or a blaring car horn, would startle him and give him a brief flashback of the explosion. He fought against the sudden panic these noises would awaken, clenching his jaw and his fists and hoping Moonbeam hadn't noticed. The last thing he needed was for her to think he wasn't up to the job. He'd been a member of Project 17 for several months now, but he still felt like the new kid on the block. He still felt the need to prove himself.

The first indication Zak had that they were nearing the airport was the shivering roar of aeroplanes flying low overhead. Soon afterwards, he saw the brightly lit terminal buildings in front of them.

The driver passed the obvious drop-off zones and took a long loop around to the back of the main buildings. The car came to a halt in a quiet area where a small jet plane stood waiting.

"This is it, folks," said the driver. "Have a good flight."

"Thank you," said Moonbeam, climbing out and holding the door open for Zak.

He stepped out into the breezy night. Tall buildings crowded together on the far side of a stretch of dark water. The car slid away into the darkness. Two men in jumpsuits stood nearby, watching them.

"Nice plane," Zak said as Moonbeam led the way to the white steps that stood at the open door at the front of the sleek silver aeroplane. "Yours?" he joked.

"I wish," Moon said as she climbed the steps. "It's a Lear 45 – a good mid-range aircraft." She looked back at him from the doorway. "It has a cruise speed of 800 kph, a range of over 3,000 kilometres and a service ceiling of fifteen and a half thousand metres." She lifted an eyebrow. "Impressed?"

"Very," said Zak.

"You haven't seen anything yet." She disappeared inside and Zak bounded up the stairs behind her.

He stopped. Staring. The executive armchairs that filled the passenger cabin were of luxurious tan leather. Zak counted just eight of them. There were side-tables of dark wood. There was even an expensive-looking carpet on the floor.

"All for us?" he asked.

Moon nodded. "Pick a seat," she said. "We'll be leaving shortly."

Zak chose a seat with a good window view.

Moon pointed to him. "Strap yourself in," she said. "Once we're in the air, you'll find food and drink in the locker at the back."

Zak frowned at her. "Where are you going?"

She hooked her thumb over her shoulder. "I'm going to check out the cockpit," she said. "Seatbelt on till you hear otherwise, okay?"

Zak clicked his seatbelt closed, watching as Moon opened the cockpit door and slipped inside. He expected to hear her speaking to the pilot, but the door closed and everything went quiet.

He was tempted to get up and see what she was doing. If Moon was getting a VIP ride in the cockpit he didn't fancy being stuck back here all on his own. He was just about to unclip his seatbelt when Moon's voice echoed electronically through the cabin. "Keep it closed, Silver!"

She could obviously see him in a monitor.

"No fair," he called. "I want to see the cockpit too."

"Later, if you're good," came Moon's amused voice. "Okay. Let's take this baby for a ride!" A moment later the jet engines roared into life. Zak watched lights bobbing through the window as the jet began to move along.

It gathered speed rapidly, taxiing between twin sets of ground-lights. There was a sudden turn, a pause, as though the aircraft was gathering its strength, and then they were off, picking up speed all the time, the lights flashing past now. The nose tilted up – Zak's stomach felt oddly hollow – and they were in the air.

He gazed out at the slowly receding airport lights. The

city of New York spread beneath him like ten thousand white diamonds scattered on black velvet.

Beautiful. Strange. And thrilling.

The small jet plane banked and headed over dark water.

Zak's excitement was tempered by apprehension. The guys who were after Alexi Roman meant business – in the worst possible way. What kind of trouble might be waiting for them when they arrived in Miami?

CHAPTER **FIVE**

"You can undo your seatbelt now," said Moonbeam's voice over the intercom.

They had been in the air for about fifteen minutes and already Zak was getting bored with the view from the window. They were over open water under a starless sky and all he could see below them in the night was featureless darkness.

He released the belt catch and stood up, stretching cautiously, feeling the protest of his aching muscles. He really hoped no one would be needing him to do any *zone* running for a while.

He made his way to the rear of the cabin and opened some doors. There was a selection of wrapped sandwiches and some silver foil boxes that he assumed went into the microwave oven that was behind another of the doors. There was a small refrigerator with bottled water and milk and some shakes and coke cans.

"All mod cons," he murmured to himself. He lifted his voice. "Hey, Moon – you coming back for something to eat?"

"That probably wouldn't be a great idea," came Moonbeam's voice. "How about you bring me a sandwich?"

"What kind?" Zak called.

"Surprise me."

Zak picked a couple of well-filled sandwiches and walked along to the cockpit door. "Can I just come in?" he asked.

"Why not?"

Zak opened the door. He gazed at the banks of dials and levers and instruments that blinked and flashed lights at him from between the two pilot seats.

Moonbeam was in the left-hand seat, her hands on the half-moon-shaped wheel of the joystick, a set of headphones on her head.

The other seat was empty.

"Moon?" he asked cautiously. "Where's the pilot?"

She turned her head and grinned at him. "You know that course I've been on for the past three months?" she said. "This is what I was learning."

Zak gaped at her. "But you're . . . what? Sixteen?" he gasped.

"Nearly sixteen," she corrected. "And Project 17 people are special, Silver. You should know that better than anyone."

A voice crackled in her ear.

"This is Washington Air Traffic Control Centre calling Flight P17."

"P17 hearing you five by five, ZDC," Moonbeam replied in a crisp, clear voice. "Go ahead."

"Flight P17," came the crackling voice. "You are maintaining agreed vector and speed protocols and you have clearance to enter ATOPS sector 66. Clear weather ahead on V414."

"Roger that, ZDC," said Moonbeam, reaching forward and flicking a few switches.

Zak gazed at Moon with new respect. He hadn't understood a word of the exchange. "Wow!" he said, handing her a sandwich.

She grinned up at him. "Pretty cool, huh?" She motioned to the co-pilot's seat. "Care to join me?"

"You bet!" Zak settled into the seat next to Moon, looking around at the baffling arrays of instruments. "Do I get a go?" he asked.

Moon grinned widely. "In your dreams," she said. She adjusted the half-moon joystick wheel and Zak watched digital numbers whirl as the plane cut its way through the night sky like a silver arrow.

"Are we there yet?" Zak asked with a grin.

"Next time you ask that, I'm slinging you out," said Moon. "Final warning!"

They were over two hours into the flight. According to Moon's calculations, they should reach Miami International Airport in another thirty minutes. Every now and then, she would receive some instructions over her headphones, but otherwise the journey had been uneventful.

Zak was doing his best to hide the feeling of apprehension that knotted his stomach as they neared their destination.

Terrorists with bombs.

Not good.

They hadn't heard from Fortress or from the FBI, not since they'd been told that Alexi's flight to London had taken off. He must be halfway across the Atlantic now. Lucky guy. Flying away from trouble instead of towards it.

An electric crackling filled the cockpit. The indicator lights flickered, plunging Zak and Moonbeam in and out of darkness. He heard the jet engines stutter.

"Uh-oh . . ." murmured Moon, leaning forward to flick some switches.

Zak looked at her uneasily. "Problems?" he asked.

"I don't know," Moon said. "It was as if there was some kind of power outage."

Then the lights blazed strongly and the roar of the engines was steady again

"Phew!" breathed Moon. "I was worried for a . . ."

The lights went out as though someone had closed the lid on a box. Zak could see nothing. *Nothing!*

The engines coughed and went dead.

Through the pitch black, he could hear Moon hissing curses and wrestling with the controls. An eerie howling, rushing sound filled his ears. His stomach lurched as the plane dipped forwards.

"*Moon* . . . ?" His heart almost stopped as he yelled into the terrifying darkness. "*Moo-oon . . . !*"

Her voice cracked in the darkness. "We're going down! There's nothing I can do. We're going down!"

07:14 UK TIME.
FORTRESS.

Bug awoke to the rattling trill of a Leopard Frog. He sat up and reached for his Mob. A red alarm was flashing. Something was wrong.

He pulled on some clothes and ran barefoot to his office. He slammed on the light with the flat of his hand and threw himself into his chair, snatching his cordless keyboard, his fingers finding the keys almost before his eyes had focused on the screens.

One of the screens showed an air traffic control display of the Eastern Seaboard of the USA. A line of green dots stretched from New York, moving in a graceful curve over the Ocean towards Miami. But the line had stopped and a red warning beacon was flashing on-screen.

Bug pressed his earpiece in place and typed again, opening a channel to Colonel Hunter.

A voice sounded in his ear. "What's wrong, Bug?"

Bug's voice was high and wavering. "They've gone off GPS, Control," he said. "Silver and Moon – their plane has . . . vanished."

"Are you picking up their ELT signal?" asked the Colonel. There was no sound of panic or alarm in his voice. The emergency locator transmitter was fitted into every aircraft. It was designed to send out a distress call if something went wrong. It activated automatically if there was a problem and could withstand virtually any kind of impact if an aeroplane went down.

"No," Bug said, typing furiously. "There's nothing."

Now a note of concern entered the Colonel's voice. "There must be a computer malfunction. Have you checked it, Bug?"

"Yes, everything's working perfectly," said Bug. His voice trembled. "The ELT isn't there, Control. They were out over the open ocean, hundreds of kilometres from anywhere. How is anyone going to find them if there's no signal to follow?"

Zak clung to his seat, listening helplessly as the wind whistled shrill and deadly around the plunging aeroplane. His heart was hammering, sending the blood through his head like pulsing drums. His instinct was to run, but there was nowhere to run to. A sour taste like rusty iron filled his mouth. Dark red flashes rimmed the blackness in front of his aching eyes. His fingers were biting into the edge of his seat. The plane was tumbling out of the night sky. He was sure he was going to die.

He felt Moon's fingers close, vice-like, on his arm. He

turned his head but saw nothing but a rim of leaping red fire.

Then, miraculously, a fierce green light erupted in the cabin. His eyes narrowed at the sudden brightness. Moon was holding a glow stick. It was slightly bent where she had twisted it to break the containers of phenyl oxalate and hydrogen peroxide to let the two chemicals mix and react.

"All the electrics are down," she gasped, her eyes wide in the strange light. "We have to get out of here. We're going down too steeply to survive the landing." She clambered out of her seat and pushed her way through the cockpit door. "Follow me." She jammed the glow stick into her waistband and hauled herself to the fuselage door.

Zak's shoes slipped on the steep slope of carpet as he followed her. She wedged herself between the cockpit wall and the door. The plane was shuddering as it fell. Zak had never been so terrified in his life. How far had they fallen already? At any moment they might hit the water.

Then what? Would the plane be smashed to fragments by the impact? Would it scythe into the ocean and slice its way down and down into the dark, cold water, cutting them off from the air – from any chance of survival?

Moon was back-kicking the wall behind her. For a moment Zak thought she'd lost the plot, then a hatch sprang open at knee-level. Moon hauled awkwardly at a large oblong pack that filled the compartment behind the hatch.

Zak helped her yank it out. He guessed what it was. An inflatable life raft.

The idea that they might survive gave him new hope.

"The door!" Moon gasped. "Two handles. Top and bottom. Then push."

He launched himself at the door, grabbing at the upper handle and dragging it down. Then he snatched at the lower handle. He felt Moon's fingers gripping his collar. He twisted the handle and pushed.

The door burst open and suddenly everything was caught up in a howling turmoil of rushing wind. He hung in the gaping doorway, half-blinded by the screaming air.

He felt Moon push something into his hand. It was the glow stick.

"Throw it down so we can see how high we are," she shouted, almost inaudibly against the fearsome noise.

He flung the glow stick out of the door. The wind pulled it away. He watched it spinning in their wake, a crazy green glow-worm in the starless night, telling them nothing.

He leaned out further, the wind lashing his face. Moon's arm snaked around his waist. He felt a thrill that was both alarm and hope. He could see the glimmering surface of the ocean now, rising rapidly beneath them.

"The life raft!" he shouted, reaching back. "Quick!" She dragged the heavy package forwards, the fingers of her free hand holding the lanyard that would make it inflate. Zak got a grip on it and yanked it to the threshold. Bracing himself with both hands, he kicked the raft out of the aeroplane.

It was whipped away, but Moon had kept hold of the lanyard toggle, and even as it twisted and spun in the dark air, it broke open and began to expand.

The ocean was hurtling towards them. They only had seconds.

Zak swung around, grabbing at Moon's clothes with both hands as he threw himself back through the open doorway.

He heard her yelling as they fell. He felt her clinging to him.

And then, with a force that battered the breath out of his lungs, they hit the water and the deep, dark throat of the Atlantic Ocean swallowed them whole.

CHAPTER **SIX**

Colonel Hunter dressed quickly, listening to information updates in his earpiece, asking short, sharp questions every now and again as he strode rapidly to the internal door of his garage. The news he was receiving from both sides of the Atlantic wasn't good.

There was still no ELT signal from Flight P17. The last contact with the missing plane had come from a point northwest of the Bahamas. If it had gone down, it could be anywhere in a vast area of open ocean.

"Was there an explosion?" he snapped. "A bomb?"

"We have no information on that, sir," replied a voice

with an American accent.

He jabbed his thumb down on his remote and the locks on his black Lotus Élan released. "A mechanical failure?"

"Sorry, sir. No information on that, either."

Colonel Hunter forced himself not to become irritated by the matter-of-fact way his questions were being answered. "Pilot error?" he growled, opening the car door and climbing in.

"We couldn't say, sir."

His patience snapped. "What *do* you know?" he barked, pressing a button to raise the garage door.

"Contact with Flight P17 was lost at 02:09 Eastern Standard Time, sir," replied the voice, sounding a little nervous now. "Coastguards have been scrambled from COMMSTA Miami, but without any signal beacon to guide them, they won't be able to begin searching properly till first light. They'll be relying on visual contact, sir." There was a pause. "It's a big ocean, sir. Even though we have the registered flight path, the plane could have veered off course before it ditched. Rest assured, everything that can be done is being done."

"Keep me updated. I want a report every fifteen minutes." Colonel Hunter terminated the call. He started his car and drove out of the garage and into daylight.

He was about to shift gears and move onto the road, when he saw a FedEx van parked in front of his house. A man in a brown uniform was heading up his driveway, carrying a parcel.

He rolled down the window. "Is that for me?" he called.

The man walked towards him. "You Peter Hunter?" he asked.

Colonel Hunter nodded.

The man handed him the package. It was about forty centimetres by thirty-five, no more than ten centimetres deep. Relatively heavy, with an American postmark on it.

The deliveryman held out a digital device and Colonel Hunter signed for proof of delivery.

The Colonel placed the package carefully on the passenger seat next to him. He touched the screen of his Mob. A line opened to Fortress. "Bug? The package has arrived. I'm coming in with it now. I'll be there in forty minutes. Have Alpha-plus security protocols in place when I arrive." His voice lowered to a rumbling growl. "Let's not make any mistakes with this," he said as he revved the engine and guided the car out onto the road. "From what Stephen Avon said, if we mess up, we won't get a second chance."

*

Zak trod water, swirling his arms as he rose and fell on the slow swell of the ocean. His clothes were hanging heavily on him, but he had no trouble keeping his head above water. Moonbeam was close by, her hair over her white face, her mouth open wide to gulp in air.

The long fall and the bone-shaking impact on the surface were vivid in Zak's mind. That, and the long plunge through black water, trying to slow down, trying to keep a grip on Moon, trying to hold his breath while his whole chest burned with pain. He wasn't quite so sure how they had managed to struggle back to the surface, but he recalled with absolute clarity that first breath of cool air in his lungs.

He wiped water from his eyes, relieved they had both survived the fall. This was the second time his life had been in peril on this mission. He hadn't realized that being a Project 17 agent could be *this* dangerous.

A yellow light was bobbing a little way off on the choppy water.

"Over there!" he panted, spitting out sea water, and pointing towards the welcoming glow. It was coming from a beacon set on the top of the life raft. The raft had inflated and landed the right way up. An orange tent lifted from its black sides, and Zak could even make out the circular shape of the zipped-up entrance flap.

"Yes. I see it," gasped Moonbeam.

They began to swim, side by side, keeping close as they fought through the rise and fall of the waves towards the life raft.

It was an awkward, slippery climb over the raised rim of the raft. Moon was first out of the water. She unzipped the flap and ripped it open, sliding inside, and squirming around to lean over the side and haul Zak aboard. For a while, they both lay in the bottom of the raft, gasping for breath.

Then Zak sat up and stared around. His eyes were used to the darkness now, and through the round entrance he could see the wide expanse of ocean that swirled all around them.

He had heard the impact of the plane on the water, but there was no sign of wreckage nearby.

"Do you think it went straight down?" he breathed.

Moon was on her knees, busy opening a series of large pockets attached to the inside of the raft. "Maybe," she said.

Zak blew out his cheeks. "If we'd still been on board . . ."

"We weren't," said Moon, looking at him before she examined another of the pockets. "There's some fresh water and rations in here," she said. "That's a good start. And a couple of paddles and some flares. They'll probably come in handy. The GPS isn't working, which is bad news." She pushed her hand into her pocket and took out her Mob. She tapped the screen a couple of times then shook her head and shoved it back into her pocket. "Waterlogged," she muttered. "I wasn't hopeful."

"What happened up there?" asked Zak. "What went wrong?"

She looked at him. "Pretty much everything, so far as I can tell," she replied, sounding baffled. "It was as if . . . I don't know . . . as if someone threw a switch and turned off all the electrics in one go. Including the engines. Total blackout."

Zak looked at her. "You mean, as if we were hit with one of those electro-magnetic pulses you and Control were talking about at the briefing?" he asked.

She stared at him. "Exactly like that," she murmured. "Silver – you're right. That was exactly what happened. It must be. Dr Avon must have come up with a way to use the pulse as a portable weapon." She screwed up her face in frustration. "This is my fault," she hissed. "I should have checked for any weird devices on the plane. *Idiot!* But the whole thing was organized at such short notice, it never occurred to me that anyone would have time to put anything nasty onboard."

Zak had been focusing all his fears on what would be coming at him once they arrived in Miami – and all along, they'd been carrying a deadly device with them in the plane. If not for their Project 17 training, the second attempt on Alexi Roman's life would have resulted in two watery deaths.

Zak shivered at the thought of their near miss.

"How could anyone have found out about the flight?" he asked.

Moon shook her head. "I don't know," she said. "It was a secret set-up between the FBI and Project 17. Air traffic control people would have been told about it at the last moment, but even if someone there had leaked the info, how did the terrorists get the device on board the plane so quickly?" She grimaced in frustration. "I can't work it out."

It was certainly a disturbing question. But right now Zak felt they had more immediate concerns.

"Do you know where we are?" he asked.

"Last time I checked the instruments we were about a hundred kilometres off the coast of Florida." She closed her eyes as though trying to remember. "Twenty-seven degrees, forty-nine minutes and thirty-six seconds north, by seventy-nine degrees, seventy-six minutes and eighteen seconds west." Zak understood map references, he'd been taught orienteering in basic training, but those precise references meant nothing to him.

"A hundred kilometres away from land sounds a lot," he said quietly. "Can we paddle that far?"

"We can give it a try," said Moon. "Though hopefully, the coastguard will locate us pretty quickly once the sun comes up."

Zak crawled to the circular entrance and peered out. The yellow beacon reflected on the water directly beneath him. He listened to the slap of waves on the life raft.

Cold! Cold and wet and out in the middle of nowhere. He stared up at the sky. The clouds were lifting a little and a few stars glimmered here and there. And then something caught his eye.

"Moon . . . ?" he said, not quite believing what he thought he could see. "How far did you say we were from land?"

"From the mainland, about a hundred klicks," she replied. "But we're not far north of the Bahamas, so there might be some islands closer by – if we're lucky."

Zak was now quite sure of what his eyes were telling him. He looked over his shoulder at Moon. "Better to be born lucky than rich," he said, echoing the words Moon had used in the hospital.

Her eyes widening, she scrambled to his side. He pointed to a low ridge of solid darkness directly in front of them.

"An island," Moon breathed. She dived to the back of the life raft and reappeared at Zak's side with two short-handled paddles.

"Well?" she said, smiling grimly. "What are you waiting for, Silver? Let's go and check it out!"

CHAPTER **SEVEN**

As they drew closer to the island, Zak made out a long pale beach where the surf broke in rippling white curls. Beyond the beach, trees crowded thickly together. There were no lights, no signs of human habitation.

"It looks fairly small," said Moon, panting slightly as she wielded the paddle at his side. "Probably uninhabited. But once we're ashore we can gather wood – start a signal bonfire on the beach."

Right then, talk of a fire sounded good to Zak. It wasn't a cold night, but his clothes were wet and he was shivering despite the effort of paddling. He hadn't completely recovered from being almost blown up earlier that night. His body was aching for warmth and rest.

The hiss and rumble of the surf grew louder. The waves were beating on the shore more wildly than they had anticipated. There were a few hectic minutes as they struggled against the breaking rollers. They tumbled out of the raft, clinging to it to haul it ashore, fighting hard as the undertow of the ocean dragged at their feet, sucking them back.

At last they fell, gasping, onto their hands and knees on fine dry sand. The raft and its provisions were safe from the clutching tide.

Zak got to his feet. Something had caught his eye a little way along the beach. A straight dark line running down the pale sand and into the sea.

"What's that?" he wondered aloud, trudging towards it through the fine, shifting sand.

Moon was at his side as they reached the dark shape. It was a double row of wooden posts sunk into the sand. The rotted remains of planking ran along the top.

"It's a jetty of some kind," said Moon, kicking at one of the crumbling posts. "Or it *was*. It can't have been used for ages." She glanced at him. "Maybe it was built by pirates a couple of hundred years ago to bring their booty ashore. There were plenty of pirates around the Bahamas in the eighteenth century."

Zak stooped and picked up a crumpled coke can, half buried in the sand. "I know pirates drank rum," he said. "Not so sure they used coke as a mixer."

"Not big on cocktails, pirates," agreed Moon. She peered up the beach into the trees. "If someone's been here recently enough to drop a coke can, there might be people living here still." She eyed him. "You up for a bit of exploring? See if there's any sign of life?"

Zak was tired and aching and exhausted, but he still had some reserves of strength and determination. "Is there a torch in the life raft?" he asked, tossing the coke can over his shoulder and heading back the way they had come. "And we might want a machete."

"There's a torch for sure," Moon said, catching up with him. "And some other gear that might come in handy." She gave a bleak smile. "Don't know about the machete, though."

"When we get back, we should write to the life raft makers and tell them to include a machete," gasped Zak as they forced their way through the dense tangle of the forest. It was hard work, fighting through the unyielding knots of shrubbery without anything to help them cut a path.

Moon led the way. She had a bag slung over her shoulder; she'd brought the water bottles and food rations and a few other things from the raft. She was lighting the path ahead with the torch, and every now and then she would let a spiky branch slip out of her hand so that Zak had to duck quickly to avoid getting smacked in the face.

What made it even worse was that some of the trees had long curved thorns on their branches – thorns that would snag in their clothes and catch in their hair.

"Be careful of that bush to the left," Moon warned as she forged on. "It's called poisonwood. Don't touch it – it'll give you a rash like poison ivy."

Great, thought Zak. Even the trees are out to get me.

The air was thick with a pungent smell that got into Zak's nose and made his eyes water. He wasn't sure what the smell was – it was sweet and a bit sickly, but with a bitter, acrid edge to it.

And there were the noises. Most of the time they were making too much of a racket for Zak to be able to hear anything else, but whenever Moon paused, flashing the torch beam through the foliage to find the easiest way forward, Zak was aware of strange scuttlings and chirruppings and clickings and whirrings all around them – as if the whole forest was alive with unseen creatures.

"Uh-oh!" gasped Moonbeam.

"What?" It was tricky for Zak to see what was going on – Moon's body blocked off most of the torchlight, and all he could make out were leafy clumps of shrubs and trees, flickering in and out of the general darkness as she roved the beam around.

"It's getting soggy underfoot," Moon said. "I think we may be heading into a swamp."

She veered to the right. Zak followed, holding his hands up to protect his face from whipping branches. The ground was a mass of twisted and gnarled roots – it was like trying to walk on a beaten-up old mattress.

"Ugh! Wet again!" came Moon's voice. "We should go back and try another way."

Except that they soon encountered more soft, sucking ground under their feet. Whichever way they went, it led them right back to the swamp.

"Okay, I give up," Moon said, turning and flashing the torch beam into Zak's face. He lifted his hand to cover his eyes. "Oh. Sorry," she said, switching the beam away from him. "Listen, this is hopeless in the dark. Let's go back to the raft and try again in the morning."

"And if the whole of the island is one big swamp?" asked Zak.

"We revisit Plan A, and build ourselves a big bonfire on the beach," said Moon. "Then we eat our rations, drink our water and wait for one of the rescue teams to see the smoke."

"That works for me," said Zak.

There was only one problem with the plan.

"Why didn't you bring the compass?" Zak asked after they had been struggling through the forest for what seemed like a very long time.

"I forgot, okay?" replied Moon, sounding irritated. "Besides, *you* could have remembered."

Zak had no answer to that.

He kept staring up through the canopy of branches, hoping to see a change in the velvet black sky, hoping for a sign of dawn and some light to help them find their way out. So far, nothing. The night seemed determined to go on forever.

Zak stepped up to his ankles in soft wet goo. They were back in the swamp.

"Listen," said Moon, raking the torch beam low across the ground. "Let's keep going – it may not be too bad."

Ahead of them, they could see tangled root systems and misshapen trunks rising out of thick brown, scummy water that smelled very unpleasant.

With a resigned shrug, Zak took another step, then sank to his knees with a startled yell. Moon lunged forwards and grabbed him, the torchlight wheeling. Zak turned, snatching hold of Moon's outstretched hand. Trying to pull his feet clear of the mud, he lost his balance. Her fingers slid through his as he fell backwards.

Foul, stinking water engulfed him. He rose to the surface, spluttering, unable to see anything, coughing and retching as he floundered in the clutching swamp.

His feet slithered from under him and he sank a second time. His shoes were caught in a web of knotted roots under the water.

"Silver! Reach for me!" Moon's voice was shrill. The torchlight was in his eyes again. He staggered, desperate to get his feet clear of the underwater roots. Finally, he managed to pull himself loose, but only by plunging deeper into the swamp.

He blundered through shoulder-high water, straining down with his feet, desperate for solid ground, gasping for breath, spitting out the disgusting swamp water.

His flailing arm hit something solid. A thick branch that stretched out over the swamp. He grasped it with both hands, panting from the effort. Using every last ounce of strength, he dragged himself up. He hooked a leg over the branch and in a few desperate moments he was sprawled over it, his heart pounding, his breath coming in choking gasps.

"Silver?" Moon sounded frantic. The torch beam was sliding over the swamp, not finding him.

"Here!" he yelled.

The beam swung towards him.

He backed along the branch and lowered himself onto dry ground. A wide brown stretch of swamp lay between them.

"Are you okay?" Moonbeam called anxiously.

"More or less," Zak called back. "Hey, Moon?"

"Yes?"

"That was a really bad idea of yours."

"I know." Moon sounded dejected. "Can you get back?" She swept the narrow beam of torchlight over the swamp and across to the low island where Zak was stranded. "Maybe you can paddle yourself back on that log," she called.

Zak turned, wiping mud out of his eyes and squinting at the large, dark greeny-brown shape that the bright beam lit up. The log was rounded and gnarled and it had a couple of stumpy, broken-off branches on one side.

It was easily big enough for him to straddle and use to float across the swamp.

He took a step towards the log. The ring of white torchlight shifted along its length, lighting up a long lumpy shape at the near end. Zak paused, suddenly uncertain.

Was it a log?

The long shape stirred and two green lights shone out eerily in the torchlight.

Zak's heart missed a beat.

The lights were eyes.

Eyes reflecting the torchlight. Radioactive green.

Holding his breath, Zak backed away, filled with a sudden alarm.

The dark shape moved with a startling, terrifying speed, rising on four stumpy, clawed legs as it jerked forwards, its thick body swinging from side to side, its long tail swishing.

Zak stumbled backwards and fell heavily to the ground as the full-grown alligator bore down on him, its fearsome jaws gaping wide.

CHAPTER **EIGHT**

Colonel Hunter and a small group of Project 17 white coats were in a brightly lit room in the Security Level 4 area of Fortress, surrounded by high-tech scanners and detectors and portals. Level 4 was the highest grade of security.

Colonel Hunter was playing it safe. Following every possible protocol.

Before he made an attempt at opening the FedEx package, he wanted to know as much about it as possible. A metal detector had revealed that there were metallic components in the box. The box had been run through an explosives trace detection portal to make sure nothing would go boom when it was opened.

A backscatter x-ray machine gave a clear 3-D computer image of what the box contained.

It was a laptop.

The Colonel watched closely as one of the white coats manipulated the image on screen – swinging it around on every axis, allowing views from all angles, zooming in to check for any hidden wires or devices.

The complex inner workings of the laptop were clearly visible on the screen.

"Anything strike you as curious, ladies and gentlemen?" asked Colonel Hunter. "Anything unusual or out of the ordinary?"

The white coats leaned closer, scrutinizing the slowly revolving x-ray image.

"Nothing obvious, Control," said a dark-haired woman. "Can you tell us what we're looking for?"

"No," said Colonel Hunter. "I can't. I don't even know if there's anything to find. But keep looking. When you're one hundred and fifty per cent certain there's nothing suspicious in the package, give me a call and we'll open it up."

One of the white coats turned to ask another question, but the Colonel was already gone.

*

Yelling in panic, Zak kicked out wildly, propelling himself backwards on his hands and heels. All he could see were rows of deadly teeth and a long red throat, lit up with horrible clarity by Moon's torch beam. The alligator was almost on him. He could hear Moonbeam calling frantically from across the swamp water.

By some miracle, and spurred on by absolute terror, Zak managed to get to his feet just as the jaws came crashing together a fraction from his ankle. He stared around. He was surrounded by trees and shrubs – there was no clear escape path. This was one time when his speed couldn't help him.

But he could climb. He launched himself into the air, snatching at the branch of a slender tree. He snapped a quick look down. The alligator reared up, its jaws gaping, its eyes glowing.

Zak pulled his feet away just in time. The alligator fell back, its heavy tail lashing to and fro. For a moment it didn't move, almost as if it was thinking about its next move.

What? That's crazy. Alligators don't think. They work on instinct. Hungry. See Zak. Grab Zak. Eat Zak.

The startling speed with which the huge creature lunged forwards took Zak by surprise again. But this time it wasn't after him – this time its jaws closed on the trunk of the tree from which Zak was dangling.

With alarming force and ferocity, the alligator shook the tree, almost jerking Zak out of his precarious perch.

He heard the crunch of breaking wood. He felt the tree shudder and begin to tip over in a rush of falling branches. The alligator had nearly bitten right through the trunk. Another few seconds and Zak would be sprawling on the ground again. Easy prey.

A point of blindingly bright red light ignited on the far side of the water and came shooting across, hissing and spitting. It hit the ground at the side of the alligator's head, showering sparks.

It was a flare.

The alligator backed away, jaws snapping. The flare spluttered and burned, its flame shrinking as the damp earth got into it.

Moon fired a second flare. It made a burning arc over the water, landing in front of the alligator's snout, blazing furiously.

The alligator twisted around and slithered away into the brown water. There was a glimpse of a low greeny-brown back, a flick of a heavy tail, and it was gone.

Zak's tree came crumpling down. He scrambled out of the tangle of branches and stood staring across at

Moonbeam. She shone the torch into his face.

"You okay?" she called.

"Spectacular," he replied breathlessly. "Thanks."

"No problem. Can you get back?"

Zak nodded. "I'll swim," he said. He checked that there were no more *logs* lying around, then waded into the swamp, moving as quickly as possible, half-expecting at any moment that long sharp teeth would sink into his leg and drag him under. He'd seen TV programmes about what alligators did to their prey.

It wasn't nice.

Moon helped him out of the scummy water. They looked at one another in heavy silence for a few moments.

"We have to get out of here," said Moon.

"We do," Zak agreed.

By some stroke of blind luck, they managed to get clear of the swamp and onto higher, drier land. But the forest was merciless, closing in around them, making them fight for every step. Zak longed for the sound of waves on the beach, for some sign that they were heading in the right direction.

As they struggled on, they were unaware of the cameras, mounted high in the trees, cameras that turned to follow them, cameras whose lenses whirred softly as they zoomed in on the two of them.

Cameras that were very interested in where they were going.

The battle with the forest would never end. They'd drunk most of their water. They were dirty and sweaty, and Zak reeked of swamp. Their strength and will-power were waning. They'd be found dead here – if they were ever found at all.

"*Yesssss!*" Moon let out a sudden screech of triumph that almost lifted Zak out of his shoes. The beam of torchlight had hit a flat white surface through the trees.

A wall. A high stone wall.

They forced their way towards it.

Walls meant people. People meant they'd survive.

The wall was too high to climb. It was white, slightly curved, running out of sight in both directions.

"Left or right?" asked Moon.

"Don't care," Zak replied. They headed left along the wall. After about fifty metres they came to thick pillars and a pair of black wrought-iron gates. Although whatever lay beyond was in absolute darkness, Zak could just about make out squareish shapes in the distance. Buildings for sure.

The gates were locked and there was no bell or obvious way of making their presence known.

"Climb," said Zak.

The scrollwork designs of the black iron gate made it relatively easy to clamber up and over the top. They jumped down onto a floor of packed gravel. Moon flicked the beam of her torch ahead.

They were in a large open compound of some kind. About twenty metres away, the white walls and windows of a sprawling, low-rise building with a tiled roof shone out in the torchlight. Towards the back, glimmering grey where the beam could not quite reach, Zak saw a squat tower with a domed roof.

"So, now what?" Zak murmured.

"We go and wake them up!" said Moon. She had only taken a single step when a whole series of floodlights burst into life, bathing them in a blindingly white glare. They fell back against the gates, their arms up to protect their eyes.

An amplified voice blared out.

"Do not move. You are trespassing on private property. Put your hands behind your heads and kneel down."

"Hey!" yelled Moon. "We're lost. Our plane ditched in the sea."

Zak peered through his fingers, unable to make out anything in the brightness of the lights.

The voice came again. "Put your hands on your heads and kneel down. Any refusal to comply will be met with extreme force."

Zak saw two shapes moving forwards against the light. Two men.

"Do as he says," Zak murmured to Moon. "They're armed."

The two men were carrying automatic machine pistols, and they were aiming the guns straight at them.

Zak and Moon dropped to their knees and laced their fingers over their heads.

"What is this place?" Moon hissed under her breath.

"I don't know," said Zak. "But they don't like visitors."

CHAPTER **NINE**

The two armed men loomed over Moonbeam and Zak, their weapons hanging from shoulder straps, the muzzles pointing menacingly at their heads.

"No, no, no!" boomed a deep voice. "This will never do. What must these poor people think of us?" A broad shape came striding forwards, arms stretched wide. "Are we barbarians? Are we uncivilized? Put those weapons away!"

The two gunmen lowered their weapons as a third man stepped between them. His arms reached down, huge, beefy hands open towards Zak and Moon.

Moon took the offered hand, but Zak got to his feet unaided. The man was big and solidly built, dressed in a white linen suit. His broad, tanned, smiling face was half-hidden by a grizzled beard, and his dark eyes flashed. His long greying hair was swept back off his forehead, thick and curling like a lion's mane.

"Forgive my people," said the man, showing rows of white teeth as he smiled. "They do not think." There was a strong accent. Zak guessed Greek.

"Our plane went down," said Moon, throwing her arm back over the forest. "In the sea."

The man's face registered shock and dismay. "No!" He looked closely at them. "You poor young people. How terrible for you. Were there other survivors?"

"There wasn't anyone else," said Zak. "Just us."

"Then that is a blessing," said the man. He slapped his hand to his chest. "My name is Spyros Milos. I am the owner of this island, and this is my home – the villa Eldorado."

"Bethany Jay," said Moonbeam. "I was the pilot." She lifted her hand. "Before you say anything, I'm not as young as I look – and I'm fully qualified."

"I'm sure you are, my dear, I'm sure you are," said Milos.

Zak had a moment to wonder if Bethany Jay was Moon's real name or just another cover, before Spyros

Milos turned enquiringly to him. A stunned look came over the man's face and his eyes opened wide. "But I know you, my young man," he gasped. "You are Alexi Roman, are you not? The brilliant young pianist. I have seen your picture many times. I have your music on my computer." A dreamy look came into his eyes. "Ahh! Your playing is sublime, my young friend." His hand came up to his heart. "You touch my very soul."

Zak blinked at him. "Thanks," he said, only just remembering to mimic Alexi's accent. "That's very kind of you."

He saw Moon flash him a quick look as if to encourage him to keep up the cover story. He didn't need telling. Until he was one hundred per cent certain that the real Alexi was safe and secure in Fortress, it was still his duty to act the part of the young musician, no matter what the circumstances.

Spyros Milos's forehead creased. "But I do not understand, my young friends – what were the two of you doing all alone in a small aeroplane?" He looked anxiously at Zak. "You are on tour in America – I know this. Where is your manager? Where are your people? Why do they let you travel alone? How does such a great talent come to fall from the sky and arrive soaked to the bone on my little island? Is it fate? Are the gods playing tricks?"

"The flight was last-minute," said Moon. "Alexi's manager wanted him to get to Miami as quickly as possible so he could rest before the next concert. The others are travelling down by train."

"Ahh, then it is fate that has brought you safely to my door!" said Milos, clapping his big hands together and smiling again. "But you are wet and muddy, my friend. You have had difficulties in the forest, I see that."

"There was an alligator," Zak said. "It tried to eat me."

Mr Milos put his hands to his mouth. "No!" he gasped. "Oh, I would never have forgiven myself. You could have lost a hand!" He turned, putting a heavy arm around each of their shoulders and walking them towards the lights. "I find the alligators useful as . . ." He paused a moment as though choosing his words. ". . . guard dogs. I am a very private man. I need my solitude. Without solitude I could not do my work. I have much work to do."

"You need armed guards to protect you as well?" asked Moon.

"Emil and Giorgio? You should not be alarmed by them. They would not have harmed you. They are . . . as you would say . . . for show. I cannot have people coming here and disturbing me." His meaty hands squeezed their shoulders. "But for two young people in such distressing circumstances, I make the exception, isn't it?" He beamed at Zak. "And for such a great talent, I throw my doors open wide, why not? Yes indeed, you shall enjoy my hospitality." His eyebrows knitted. "But you said your aeroplane crashed – how did such a thing happen?"

Moon hesitated for a moment. "Electrical failure," she said.

"Ahh." Mr Milos looked thoughtful. "Electrical failure? How strange you should say that. What a terrible thing!"

"I'm sorry, but what we need right now is a telephone," said Moon. "We have to call people – let them know we're okay."

Mr Milos's face fell. "I wish you had asked for anything else, my young friend," he said. "It is a most extraordinary thing. You will not believe it, I am sure, but everything in my home that is powered by electricity has also failed. It happened no more than three hours ago. Everything went quite dead! It is most perplexing." He looked into Moon's face. "It is strange that everything electrical on this island should fail, and that your plane should suffer a similar problem."

"Weird," said Moon guardedly. "Maybe it was some kind of atmospheric phenomenon? An electrical storm shorting everything out?"

"Yes. Maybe so," mused the big man. "You may be correct."

"Your floodlights still seem to be working," Zak remarked.

"They have a special dedicated circuit fed by an emergency alkaline battery system which mercifully was not affected," Mr Milos said. "Everything else in my home is dead!' He led them to a set of steps that took them up to a veranda. "You see?" he said. "No lights. No music. No life at all. My computers are down. It is very inconvenient. I cannot work."

"Do you usually work in the middle of the night?" asked Moon.

Mr Milos smiled broadly. "I have business interests all over the world, my young friend," he said. "For a man such as myself, the sun never sets." He drew them into a candlelit lounge. Even in the dimly flickering light, Zak could see that Mr Milos liked his luxuries.

"Now, before we do anything else, you must clean yourselves up," said Mr Milos. "We shall have to find you some fresh clothes. I have some garments that may fit you. My children sometimes come to visit for a short while, and clothes are left here for them. I am afraid I have no maids or house servants, but Emil and Giorgio will help you find your way." He smiled. "They are as gentle as puppies once you get to know them."

Zak had seen the glint in the eyes of the two men as they had stood over them with guns at the ready. He doubted very much that either of them was as gentle as a puppy. Except perhaps a psychotic puppy. All the same, a good wash and a change of clothes sounded great.

He gave Moon a private glance and she returned a brief nod.

"And when you are clean and refreshed, you must rest," said Mr Milos. "You must be exhausted. Dawn is not far off, but you shall have a few hours' sleep." He spread his hands. "Who knows? In the morning, the electrical troubles may correct themselves and all will be well."

"I hope so," said Moon. "We really need urgently to make contact with the outside world."

"As do I, my friend," sighed Mr Milos. "As do I."

Zak lay in bed, curled up under clean, fresh sheets. He felt so weary that he could hardly find the strength to yawn, but there was a bright light in his brain that wouldn't let him sleep.

Mr Milos had asked Emil to show him to a guest bedroom in one wing of the huge villa, while Giorgio led

Moonbeam off in another direction. Emil didn't seem to speak much English, communicating mostly with gestures. Moving through the corridors by torchlight, Zak was shown to a pleasant bedroom with en-suite bathroom. Emil opened a wardrobe, revealing a whole lot of clothes that Zak thought would probably fit him. Emil had opened the window, indicating to Zak that it would be too hot in the room otherwise, and then left Zak to it.

Zak had showered, dried himself, thrown on some loose-fitting pyjamas from the wardrobe and crashed into bed. At some point he would need to huddle with Moon and figure out what to do next – but right now he just wanted to sleep. He really deserved it!

Except sleep wouldn't come.

The events of the past few hours kept replaying themselves in his head. Dr Avon's frightened face on video. Alexi laughing when he saw Zak's disguise. The red flare of the bomb and the sickening lurch of the explosion. The sudden darkness coming down in the plane like an iron shutter. The alligator. The men with the guns. Mr Milos's huge smile.

The images played over and over on a continuous loop.

Driving him crazy.

Sleep? Where are you? Come on – it'll be light soon!

A small sound caught his attention in the darkness. A furtive noise near the open window. If not for the absolute silence in the villa he would not have noticed it.

He went rigid, all his attention now focused on listening. A creak, soft as a whisper, but somehow menacing. He swivelled his eyes, trying to pierce the blackness. Yes! There was something – by the window – he could just make out a stooped shape against the very first hint of dawn light.

He sat up. "Who's there?"

There was a flurry of sound and Zak saw the hunched shape lift itself swiftly onto the frame of the window and jump into the night.

He scrambled out of bed and bounded over to the window. He saw a dark shape running alongside the building. In a moment the figure had vanished around a corner. It was Emil – he was sure of it. But what had he been doing climbing into Zak's room?

There was no time to get dressed, but Zak didn't like the idea of chasing the interloper without some kind of defence. He grabbed the lipstick-sized Kiss that he had stashed under his pillow for safe-keeping, then he ran to the window and sprang down onto thick grass. He sprinted to the corner, moving as quietly and as quickly as he could, holding the Project 17 sleeping-drug injector tight in his fist. The hem of the sky was silver-grey now with the coming day. He risked a quick glance around the corner.

He stared down a long stretch of featureless wall. No way had he given Emil the time to run to the far end. But there was no sign of him. Puzzled, Zak slipped around the corner and ran on.

His bare toes snagged on something. A raised edge. He crouched, examining it. His eyes widened in surprise. A whole section of turf was lifted slightly – there was a narrow gap. Zak forced his fingers into the gap and hauled upwards. A two metre square of turf rose on a hinge like some kind of trapdoor. It was heavy, but Zak managed to get his shoulder under it to support it.

He found himself looking down a shadowy flight of concrete steps. In the gloom at the bottom, he could just make out a metal door.

There was no way of holding the hatch open while he investigated further, but he was absolutely certain that Emil must have gone through that door. That was the only explanation for how he could have vanished so quickly.

Zak let the heavy hatch shut again. He stood, thinking hard. Obviously, Emil had been sneaking about in his room. But why? All of Zak's instincts, all of his Project 17 training, every fibre in his body told him that there was something very wrong about this. Something dangerous. He just couldn't work out *what*.

Forget sleep. He'd go and find Moonbeam. Fill her in on what had happened. Maybe she'd be able to make sense of it.

He ran to his window and clambered back in. The silvery light was filtering into the room now, giving everything a strange, ghostly look. He was about to run to the door when he heard a sharp hissing.

He stopped, not liking the sound, and stared at the floor.

A long slender shape was gliding in undulating loops across the carpet towards him. A narrow, wedge-shaped head rose. Zak saw two points of light staring up at him.

Snake.

He looked at the approaching creature in breathless disbelief.

As though in slow motion, the snake reared up in front of him. It drew its head back for a moment, parted its jaws to reveal needle-sharp fangs, and then, with sudden, deadly speed, it struck.

CHAPTER **TEN**

Instinct, training and speed all came together in an instant. Zak flexed his knees and sprang high above the snake's head, his legs tucked underneath him, his arms stretched for balance.

He came down lightly behind the snake, his eyes focused on the creature's head. It spun round like a lashing whip, jaws agape. Zak was in the air again before the snake could strike. He landed on the edge of the bed and slipped, falling so that his head and shoulders hung over the side.

For a split second, he found himself staring into the

snake's cold black eyes. A hiss. A dart forwards. He flung himself back and the snake's fangs sank into the bedclothes.

Scrambling up the bed, Zak grabbed a pillow and fought to get the pillowslip loose. The snake was sliding onto the bed now. Zak held the pillowslip open between his two hands, watching the snake, hardly breathing. Its head lifted again – but this time Zak was ready. He lurched towards the snake, bringing the pillow slip down over its head. He reached out, shoving the rest of the body into the bag, then lifted the whole squirming thing into the air.

Panting with shock and fear, he climbed off the bed and ran for the en-suite bathroom. He sent the writhing bag skidding across the floor then slammed the door on it.

Zak sat with his back against the door, getting his breath back. A connection formed in his brain. Emil at the window – a snake in his room.

Coincidence?

I don't think so.

He stood up and ran to the bedroom door. He had to find Moonbeam. Something was going on here – and they needed to figure out what to do about it.

*

Zak crept through the huge villa. The dawn was breaking, sending long beams of silvery light through the large windows. He was wary, hyper-alert, listening for the faintest sound.

He came to a descending flight of stairs. He paused, staring down at the light that came from the crack of a part-open door.

What's wrong with this picture?

Electric lights, that's what's wrong.

He glided down the stairs, pressing himself to the wall as he stole a brief glance through the gap.

Spyros Milos was sitting at a desk dominated by four large plasma screens. There was a keyboard in front of him and he was wearing a slim-line wireless headset. Four faces stared out from the screens. Three men and a woman. Zak didn't like the look of them at all.

So much for his computers being down.

"I think you can do better than that," Mr Milos was saying. "I have been to considerable trouble and expense to make this product available on the open market."

One of the men spoke. "Twenty-eight million in gold."

"You make fun with me, no?" said Mr Milos. He got up, his voice becoming angry. "You think I am the fool, is that it? You all wish to play the games with me?" He stepped towards the desk again. "I will give you all some time to think seriously about your offers. Goodbye, for the moment. Gentlemen, madam." He pressed a key and the screens went blank, then he turned to the door, muttering furiously to himself.

Zak ducked away, thinking hard.

Maybe the electrics had been fixed overnight?

Or maybe they had never been down at all. Which would mean that Spyros Milos had been lying to them.

But why?

He needed to find Moonbeam – and quick. He padded up the stairs and continued his search through the sprawling villa.

He found her room after a few minutes, and without encountering anyone else. She wasn't asleep. She was sitting cross-legged on the bed, dressed in borrowed jeans and T-shirt that were slightly too big for her.

"Good," she said as Zak slid into her room. "I was just about to go and look for you. We need to discuss the situation we're in." She frowned, seeing the expression on his face. "What's wrong?"

Zak told her the breathless story of Emil and the snake and the turfed-over hatchway that led to the underground door. Then he filled her in on seeing Mr Milos in the fully functional basement office. Busy with a video-link conference call.

It was a lot for her to take in.

"The snake thing is bad," Moon said thoughtfully. "Let's think this through. If Milos wants you dead . . ."

"Wants Alexi Roman dead," Zak corrected her.

She nodded. "Wants *Alexi* dead, why not just shoot you the moment he sees who he thinks you are?"

"Beats me," said Zak. "But why would he want Alexi dead at all?"

"That's the million dollar question," said Moonbeam. She frowned deeply. "Is Milos somehow involved with the people who kidnapped Dr Avon? The same people who are trying to silence Alexi?" She shook her head. "No! That's crazy. This island is a just a dot in the Atlantic – there's no way in the world we would fall out of the sky right here . . ." Her eyes widened. "Unless we were taken down *on purpose* right here. Was the EMP device timed to activate close to this island? But why? If the idea was to kill you in the crash, what does it matter where it happens?" She pressed her hands on either side of her head. "This is making no sense! What's going on?"

"Whatever it is, we need to get away from this place," insisted Zak.

She looked at him. "And go where, exactly?" she asked. "Back to the life raft? Do you know which way that is, because I don't." Her voice was firm. "No, dangerous as it is, we need to stay here and play along till we have a better idea of what Milos and his pals are up to."

"They're trying to kill Alexi," Zak said. "That's what they're up to."

"Very probably," agreed Moon. "But they seem to want to make it look accidental, don't they? Killed in the night by a snake bite. Think about it, you could be dead ten times over if they didn't care how it looked. Milos is trying to cover his back. The only reason to do that is if he's not sure whether anyone knows we survived the crash. If the search and rescue teams come here, he wants to be able to act innocent."

"So, what do we do?" asked Zak.

"We play the whole thing by ear. Don't let Milos know we're suspicious. We need to try and find out what's going on – and we need to find a way either to communicate with the outside world, or to get off this island undetected."

"And I'd like to know what's on the other side of that secret underground door," Zak added.

"You and me both," Moon said. "We'll check that out the first chance we get. But right now, we need to be smart – and act dumb. So, Alexi has just woken up to find a snake in his room. What would he do?"

"He'd freak!" said Zak.

Moon's eyes narrowed. "So, go freak!"

"My dear young friends, I am mortified by what nearly happened under my own roof!" gasped Mr Milos. "I have lived here many years, and never before has a snake come into the house." He put a hand on Zak's shoulder. "Are you entirely recovered, Alexi?"

"I'm fine, Mr Milos, thank you," said Zak.

"You were very brave to trap the reptile like that," said Mr Milos. "You are a resourceful young man."

If Spyros Milos was acting, he deserved an Oscar.

So did Zak. He had run through the corridors, screaming his head off. "Snake! Snake!"

Mr Milos and his henchmen had appeared and Zak had taken them back to his room, playing the part of someone half out of his mind with panic. Emil had been told to dispose of the creature, and Mr Milos had taken Zak and Moonbeam out onto the veranda, which overlooked a kidney-shaped blue swimming pool sparkling in the light of the rising sun. He seated them at a table and instructed Giorgio to make them all an early breakfast.

"Any luck getting the electricity back on, Mr Milos?"

asked Moon, as they ate bowls of Greek yogurt with muesli and honey. Zak was impressed at how innocent she managed to make the question sound.

"Alas not," said Mr Milos, sighing. "All is still dead. It is most aggravating."

You total liar!

"It must be," said Zak, looking at him closely. "No computers, no phone lines. And I don't suppose you have a mobile phone that works either?"

Mr Milos shook his head and threw his hands up. "What is a businessman to do?" he exclaimed. "But Emil and Giorgio are working on it. They are hopeful that the electricity will be flowing very soon."

"Then we can make a call to let everyone know we're all right," said Moon. "Ask them to send a boat to pick us up."

"That is something I will certainly do at the very first moment the electricity is back,' said Mr Milos, beaming.

"You must have a boat on the island, Mr Milos," said Zak. "Is it moored nearby?"

"It is at the far end of the island," said Mr Milos. "Come, if you are finished eating, I will show you a map."

He took them into a long sunlit room. There was a large framed map of the island on the wall.

Mad Cat Cay.

"Mad Cat Cay is really two islands linked by a high and very narrow causeway," Mr Milos explained. "Mad Cat – an amusing name, is it not? I don't know why it's called that." The map showed two teardrop-shaped islands, joined at the points by a thin stretch of land. He tapped his finger on the northern part of the island. "We are here," he said, tracing his finger over the causeway to the southernmost tip, where the island threw out two claws to make a perfect little harbour. "My boats are moored here – it is quite a distance, but nowhere else affords such a secure harbour. We have some ATVs – quad bikes – which we use to get around the island." He smiled. "They are very useful. Sometimes Emil and Giorgio, they like to race them on the beaches. I indulge them, why not?"

"So, if you can't get the electrics working, we could always use one of your boats," said Moon. "To take us to the mainland?"

"Of course we will," said Mr Milos. "But first we give Emil and Giorgio a little while longer to fix our problem, yes?" He gave them another of his wide toothy smiles. "In fact, I will go and find them right now and see how they are getting along." He snapped his fingers. "We will have it all fixed like that, you will see. Maybe you two young people would like to make use of the swimming pool while you wait? You will find bathing costumes in your rooms." He clapped his hands together. "Yes. You swim and relax while we work to give you electricity. How does that sound?"

"It sounds perfect, Mr Milos," said Moon with a wide smile. "For someone who doesn't like guests, you're a brilliant host."

Mr Milos beamed. "For Alexi Roman and his friend, I do all that I can," he said. He looked at Zak. "And in a little while perhaps Alexi will repay me?"

Zak gave him a puzzled look. "Excuse me?"

"I have a piano," Mr Milos explained. "Perhaps Alexi will condescend to play for me later this morning? I would so love that!"

"Oh, yes . . ." stammered Zak. "Of course . . . no problem . . ."

"Excellent!" cried Mr Milos. "And now I leave you." He lifted a finger. "Please do not stray beyond the walls of Eldorado," he warned them gently. "In the forest lurk many dangers – snakes and alligators, as you already know. And other perils – such perils for the unwary! I would not wish you to come to harm."

"We'll stay right here," said Moon.

"Then I will return shortly," he said. "Hopefully with good news." He strode out of the room, leaving them gazing at one another.

"Okay," Moon murmured. "Let's get busy."

FORTRESS.
SECURITY LEVEL 4.

Colonel Hunter made sure Bug was in the room when the package from Stephen Avon was finally opened.

The Colonel lifted the laptop out of the cardboard FedEx box and carefully unwrapped the rolls of bubble-wrap. He set the laptop on a desk and stepped back.

Bug moved in, sitting down and opening the laptop. He booted it up and began attaching cables and leads to various USB ports, glancing at the monitor screens on the desk to check the results.

The Colonel watched tensely for several minutes while Bug typed, paused, checked the various screens, then typed again, all in total silence.

"Dr Avon said something about a key," said Colonel Hunter under his breath. "Can you work out what he meant by that?"

"I'm pretty sure he meant it's password protected," said Bug. "I've got a transcript of Alexi's statement about his encounter with Dr Avon – I'm going to use a lot of different combinations of the words Dr Avon used when he was talking to Alexi. I'm trying some complex algorithms right now – they should give me a codeword without frying the hard drive." He glanced up at the Colonel. "There's no way he came up with a password I can't find," he said.

The Colonel nodded, but his face was pensive.

A few tense minutes went by.

"Uh oh," muttered Bug. A moment later the laptop screen erupted in a zigzag dazzle of black and white lines then went blank.

"What happened?" Colonel Hunter asked, his voice oddly calm.

"I messed up," breathed Bug. He looked around at the Colonel. "Good news or bad news?"

"Give me your report, Bug," said the Colonel.

"I've managed to download about half the files onto an external hard drive," said Bug. "But the rest were protected by a firewall that was more sophisticated than I'd thought."

"Meaning you can't get in?" growled the Colonel.

"Oh, I'll get in all right," muttered Bug. "But it'll take a while – and I'm not sure how much has survived. I may have fried up to nine-tenths of the motherboard. It's going to be tricky." He looked up at the Colonel. "I work better undisturbed," he said quietly.

The Colonel nodded, turning to leave the room.

His Mob made a bright chiming sound. He knew the dedicated ringtone immediately.

"Switch?" he said. "You've landed? Good. I want that boy inside Fortress as soon as possible." He closed the line and pocketed his Mob. "Bug?" he barked. "Your best effort, okay? And fast."

"I'm on it, Control."

The door closed behind Colonel Hunter and Bug got to work.

CHAPTER **ELEVEN**

The grass-covered trapdoor stood open against the wall. Zak and Moon were at the bottom of the flight of steps. Moon had unrolled a small leather pouch and was working the lock of the door with a pair of slender metal picks.

"Gotcha!" she whispered. She pressed a single finger against the door and it swung open.

"How come I was never taught breaking and entering?" murmured Zak, looking enviously at the roll as she wound it up again and pushed it into her pocket.

"It's on the advanced course," Moon whispered.

"You'll get there."

The door opened onto a short corridor lit by bulkhead lights attached to the walls. All was silent down there – and strangely cool. The corridor ended at a T-junction.

"Which way?" asked Zak, staring along the two alternative routes.

"I'll go this way, you go that," Moon said, pointing left and then right. "Meet back here when we're done. Okay?"

Zak nodded.

He walked lightly along the corridor until he came to a door. He listened for a few moments then turned the handle, peering into what seemed to be a supply room, filled with boxes and tins. A little further on, he found a similar room. The next door was more interesting. It showed signs of having been forced. The frame by the lock was broken, as though someone had smashed it from the inside.

He swung the door open.

His senses were on immediate high alert. This room was quite different.

He felt for the light switch. A bare bulb ignited, filling the room with sudden harsh light. It was not a large room, and it was crammed with stuff. There was a table littered with electronic equipment, some of it apparently in fully working condition – computers and monitors and similar devices – and some of it just a scattering of bits and pieces, half made-up.

But the most curious thing to Zak was the small cabinet and the unmade single bed that lay along one wall.

It was as though someone had lived, worked and slept here.

Some clothes were crumpled in an open suitcase on the floor and there were signs of a meal that had never been finished. On the bedside cabinet stood a small radio/CD player and a few sad personal items. A couple of dog-eared photographs, a gold fob-watch, two or three scuffed and worn books, and lying open in front of the CD player – a CD case.

Zak picked up the case, an eerie sensation sending shivers down his spine. Almost before he'd looked at it properly, he knew which CD it was.

He turned it over and gazed down at the dreamy-eyed face of Alexi Roman. And written in silver ink across the cover picture was a dedication.

To my friend and my very first piano teacher, Doctor Avon, with grateful thanks and very best wishes – Alexi

It was dated almost twelve months previously.

"Dr Avon was *here*," breathed Zak, staring around the

room. "This is where he was being held captive."

He could imagine the terrible scene in his head. Dr Avon in his home, little knowing what was to come. A knock at the door – or maybe the crash of glass as a window was broken. Men in the house – two men with automatic weapons, perhaps? Emil and Giorgio. Dr Avon at gunpoint, being allowed to pack some clothes and a few precious items. Then bundled into a waiting car. An aeroplane. A boat. Frightened and bewildered – gagged – bound? Maybe struck to ensure his absolute obedience while he was taken on the long, dreadful journey to captivity in this room.

Zak frowned, trying to come up with a plausible chain of events. Spyros Milos was the person keeping Dr Avon captive – that much was obvious. He must have forced Dr Avon to complete his work and to create and construct an EMP weapon. Which surely meant Milos must be part of the terrorist group planning the attack.

Dr Avon had escaped and gone to speak to Alexi – to give him some clue that would help prevent the attack. Milos must know about the meeting – and that was why he wanted Alexi dead. Yes, that *must* be it.

Zak moved swiftly to the desk, leaning over the computer, pressing the button to start it up.

Another vivid image came into his mind. Dr Avon

sitting on the bed, perhaps, eating that unfinished meal, listening to the radio. Hearing the interview with Alexi. Discovering that his former pupil was in Miami – only a hundred kilometres away across the ocean. Hatching a desperate escape plan. Knowing his life may be in danger, but determined somehow to get to Alexi before he was recaptured. To tell him a vital secret – a secret that only Alexi would understand.

Except that Alexi hadn't understood it.

Zak grimaced as he remembered Dr Avon's terrified face on the video, and the sudden, brutal way the video had ended.

Stephen Avon had not been brought back here, then. An ominous feeling crept over Zak. Dr Avon had been caught – but where was he now? What terrible price had he paid for his escape bid?

Moonbeam glided along the corridor, moving silently, listening intently. There were no doors, no side corridors. No signs of life at all. The corridor ended in another of those metal doors.

Frowning, Moon crouched and unrolled her tools for a second time. A few seconds with the metal picks and the door was open. Her eyes widened in astonishment. The room was crammed with boxes and crates of weaponry and ammunition.

"He's got an entire arsenal down here," she breathed, slipping into the room. "*Bad* Mr Milos – what *are* you up to?" She moved among the stockpile of weapons, spotting boxes of grenades and high explosives. She stopped in her tracks, listening hard again. Was that a voice?

Her eyes tracked up the wall to a high metal vent. There was light beyond it – and yes, a voice. Spyros Milos's voice.

She climbed a stack of boxes. She could see nothing through the grille, but she could hear Mr Milos quite clearly.

"Madam, gentlemen, I can assure you, Burning Sky is fully operational and ready to be sold to the highest bidder," he was saying.

A woman spoke, her voice slightly distorted. "How do we know it will work, Mr Milos? What proof do you have?"

Moonbeam guessed that Milos was on another conference call.

"I have already tested it, my dear madam," said Mr Milos. "I used it to deal with the small hitch that arose when Dr Avon escaped. I can promise you it worked

– I operated it myself to bring down the plane that was taking the boy to Miami. The plane fell out of the sky like a stone!" A self-satisfied tone came into his voice. "I have some cutting-edge technology here. I was able to hack into Air Traffic Control and learn the exact details of their flight from New York. I watched them all the way in real time, and I was able to detonate the EMP at exactly the right moment."

"So, the boy is dead?" asked a man's voice. "And whatever Avon told him has died with him?"

"The boy survived the crash," said Mr Milos. "He is here with me now, with a female companion."

"Why have you not killed him?" asked a third voice.

"I know the plan was to kill him and be done," said Mr Milos. "But now I have him here, I would like to know exactly what Avon told him, and who *he* has told. A snake was to bite him – and I was going to withhold the antidote unless he told all." Mr Milos chuckled. "He would not have known there *was* no antidote."

"People will be searching for him," said the voice. "Kill him, and do it quickly, or I will sever all links with you, Milos."

"As will my company," said the woman. "You are being reckless."

"I will kill him if you insist," said Mr Milos. "Within

the hour, I will lead him and the young woman into the swamp at gunpoint and allow the alligators to take them."

Moon's fists clenched in anger. *Murdering swine!*

"Do it right this time," said the voice. "Your attempt to get rid of him in New York was an utter failure."

"This time he will not survive, I promise you," Milos replied.

"You ask much faith from us concerning Burning Sky," said the woman's voice. "How can we take your word that the device works?"

"You do not need to," said Milos. "Burning Sky will be given a very public debut this coming Friday. I suggest you keep tuned to the international news media and discover for yourselves how effective the device can be."

Moon heard a sound behind her. She turned, the hairs rising on the back of her neck.

Emil stood in the doorway, his eyes glittering, the muzzle of his automatic machine pistol aimed at her forehead.

Zak gazed at the computer screen. A line of blue folders ran down the left hand side. They had cryptic titles such as BS02374 or Ex.21-ap59fh-alpha.

At first he had been surprised that there was no password preventing him from opening the home screen – nothing to keep the computer secure.

"No need," he murmured as he clicked on one of the folders. "Who's going to see it down here?"

A page opened, filled with sub-folders and files. Again, the titles gave nothing away – unless you were some kind of electronics expert like Dr Avon, Zak assumed. He closed the folder and opened others, hoping for something that he could make sense of.

The fifth folder contained some JPEG images.

Click to open.

A diagram of a microchip circuit.

Another.

A schematic of a CMOS chip.

Another.

More integrated circuit chips.

Zak frowned. He had no idea what these pictures meant.

He looked around, hoping to see a memory stick or external hard drive – something that would allow him to download all this stuff and get it to someone who understood what it was all about.

There was nothing.

But he did notice that several USB leads lay unattached around an oblong on the desk that was curiously free of clutter.

"As though something was there," he murmured to himself. "Something that's been taken away?" Something about the size of a laptop.

He tapped at the JPEG files, opening dozens of them, learning nothing.

Then he saw it.

A series of photos of a device of some kind, taken from several angles. It had been photographed standing on this table. It reminded Zak of one of those expensive telescopes that people used to look at the stars. It was about forty centimetres long and maybe twenty-five in diameter, barrel-shaped, with a USB port panel at one end and an opening at the other, like the iris of a camera. The whole thing stood on a squat tripod stand and cables fed into the USB ports.

The title of the JPEG was: Burning Sky 1st prototype.

He opened the next JPEG. It showed images of a very similar device.

Burning Sky, Mark 2.

Zak's eyes narrowed in alarm. So, there were at least two of these devices in existence. That was really bad news.

A third picture showed the device from further away. The cables could now be seen feeding into a laptop computer.

He opened a diagram, showing the device apparently working. There was a list of technical data by the computer – operating instructions, Zak guessed. Dotted lines reached out in a narrow cone from the front of the device, aimed at a drawing of an aeroplane.

There was some impenetrable maths – but the thing that disturbed Zak was an arrow pointing down from the underside of the aeroplane.

The meaning was horribly clear. The device fired a narrow beam of *something* at the aeroplane – and the aeroplane went down.

Burning Sky was an EMP weapon. A sudden realization hit Zak: the device had never been on board their jet. It had been fired from here. The device was right here in this building.

Zak remembered the tower he had noticed when they had first arrived – the tower with the domed top. The perfect place for firing an EMP into the night sky.

"Milos knew we were coming," he muttered to himself. "He tested Burning Sky on us. He hoped we'd be killed."

He must have been surprised and disappointed when they'd turned up at his compound – but he'd hidden it well, pretending his own electrics had gone down so they couldn't ask him to contact anyone for help.

"Moon has to see this!"

Zak ran from the room and hurried along the corridor, moving as quietly as possible in case Milos or his henchmen were close by.

He came to a sudden halt, staring at a figure that was standing in an open doorway at the far end of the corridor.

Emil. He was holding a gun.

Zak hesitated, his palms sweating, beads of perspiration sliding down his forehead. He wasn't sure he could do this. One sound, one wrong move and he'd be staring down the bad end of a gun barrel.

But Moonbeam needed him. He mustn't doubt himself.

Swallowing hard, he moved forwards, reaching into his pocket for the Kiss.

Holding his breath, he padded up behind Emil and touched the Kiss against the side of the man's neck. He pressed the end. There was a sharp hiss. Emil spun around, his face ferocious. Before he could make another move, the light went out of his eyes and he toppled over.

Zak snatched the gun out of his hands as the man slumped to the floor.

Moon was staring down at him from the top of a big pile of wooden crates.

He was about to speak, when she put her finger to her lips and pointed to a high metal grille through which strips of light were filtering.

She climbed down, bringing her mouth close to his ear.

"Milos is in the next room," she whispered. "He's trying to sell something called Burning Sky."

Zak nodded sharply. "I know what that is," he said. "There's a computer. Loads of info. You should see it."

Moon shoved Emil aside and closed the metal door to the armaments room softly behind them. "No time," she said quietly. "He's going to have us killed – we need to get out of here." Her eyes glittered. "They'll realize Emil is missing, then they'll be after us. We need to get as far away as we can – and we need to do it fast."

"The quad bikes," said Zak. "Remember? Mr Milos said they use quad bikes. We can take a couple of them and make for the harbour down in the south of the island."

Moon nodded eagerly. "Good idea." Her eyes narrowed. "I just need two minutes to do something in there," she said, jerking her thumb towards the room full of weapons. "Stay here. Keep watch. Let me know if Giorgio comes."

She opened the door and slid inside. Zak stared impatiently along the corridor, dreading at any moment to see Mr Milos's other heavy arriving with his gun under his arm.

Moon was true to her word. Zak guessed that it was a few seconds shy of two minutes when she reappeared.

"Okay," she said. "It's done."

"What's done?" asked Zak as they ran down the corridor.

"I've set us up some insurance," she said. "Hopefully we won't need it. Come on – let's get out of here."

They found the quad bikes parked together close to a gate at the back of the compound. Keys were in the ignitions.

"Do you know how to drive one of these?" asked Moon.

Zak shook his head.

"Okay," Moon said briskly, straddling the nearest of the sturdy big-wheeled bikes. "Open the gate, then. I'll drive, you ride pillion."

Zak was hauling the gate open when he heard shots. He ducked, his whole body clenched in fear, listening to bullets whining past. He spun to see Giorgio on the veranda of the villa, firing his machine pistol again, the bullets sending up spits of gravel at Zak's feet.

He threw himself down, his hands over his head, as the deadly pistol fire churned up the ground around him.

CHAPTER **TWELVE**

Zak heard the growl of the quad bike engine and the screech of tyres on gravel.

"Get on!" yelled Moon as the quad bike skidded, spraying gravel as it sped between the gateposts.

"Stop them, you fool!" came the angry bellow of Spyros Milos's voice.

More bullets flew, digging holes in the white wall as Zak sped through the gates with his head down. Moon gunned the motor and the bike accelerated rapidly.

He ran, arms pumping, his eyes and his mind focused on the bike. Moon was shooting quick glances over her shoulder. "Way to go, Silver!" she shouted as he sped up. "C'mon!"

No problem. He was in the zone – in that special place where mind and body meshed and he could outrun lightning. He caught up with the speeding bike and leaped onto the pillion seat, wrapping his arms around Moon's waist as she twisted the throttle and the bike gave a powerful surge forwards.

A narrow road cut through the forest, running south.

As they raced along, Zak risked a quick look back.

A grey Range Rover was following – and catching up fast. Zak could see Milos at the wheel, but the scariest thing was that the top was open and Giorgio was standing, leaning on the frame of the windscreen and aiming his machine pistol right at them.

"Have you had a breakthrough, Bug?" asked Colonel Hunter as he strode into the small tech-filled office. An alert from Bug had brought him here, almost at a run.

"Kind of," Bug replied. "I've checked out the files I downloaded before my miscalculation – they're not very interesting, I'm afraid."

"And the files still on the computer when it got fried?" asked the Colonel.

"More survived than I expected," said Bug. "There were ten folders in all – and I've managed to pick the locks on nine of them." He frowned. "The tenth one is a total nightmare, though. I've tried everything I can think of, but it's still codeword locked." He gave an exasperated shake of his head. "I'm running some programs to try and get it open, but there's something screwy about the way it's been protected. It doesn't respond to anything. I can't get my head around it, Control."

"You'll get there," said the Colonel. "What did you find in the other nine folders?"

"Plenty of interesting stuff," Bug said. "Masses of data about electro-magnetic pulses and how to try and solve the problems of making a device that would be able to target a pulse on command, and not wreck everything electronic within a five-kilometre radius."

"And did Dr Avon solve the problems?"

"He did," said Bug, typing at speed so that pages came up one after the other on the plasma screens over his workstation. "According to his diary notes, he not only worked out all the software programming problems, but he managed to build the real thing." He frowned. "But here's the problem," he said. "None of these files reveal *how* he solved the problems, or how the thing actually works."

"Presumably all that information is hidden in the final folder," said the Colonel. "The one you can't get open." He frowned. "And the details of the terrorist attack must be on that file as well."

"They have to be," said Bug. "You can see how he was thinking, can't you? He hides all the info anyone would need to actually construct and use the thing in a folder that can't be opened by any of the normal decryption methods. Then he gives Alexi Roman the key to getting it open."

The Colonel nodded. "That way, if the laptop was intercepted by anyone en route, they wouldn't be able to make practical use of what they'd found."

"Would you like to see the real thing?" asked Bug. He pressed his mouse and a JPEG image of a barrel-shaped device appeared. "He calls it Burning Sky."

"Very poetic," said the Colonel. "Did he test it? Does it work?"

"Simulations worked just fine, apparently," said Bug, as more pages popped up on the screens. "Although, again, the details must be in the locked folder." Bug twisted around in his chair and looked up into the Colonel's grey eyes. "Do you know of anyone with the codename Conquistador?" he asked.

Colonel Hunter's eyes narrowed. "He's an illegal

arms dealer," he said. "Thought to be of Greek origin. There are no pictures of him and almost no Legend. The security forces of half the world would like to get their hands on him."

"Well, according to one of the files on here, Conquistador is planning to auction off Burning Sky to the highest bidder," said Bug. "And it looks as though he has some pretty nasty people on his client list. Rogue states, private armies, terrorist organizations. You name it, they're interested." Bug tapped the keyboard again. "He's going to demonstrate the weapon for them some time very soon."

"Do we know where and when?" asked the Colonel, his face grave.

Bug's shoulders slumped. "We don't," he said. "Not yet."

Colonel Hunter walked towards the door. "Let me know the moment you get that last folder open," he growled. Then he was gone.

"Will do, Control," Bug called. Then, lowering his voice, "Just don't hold your breath while you're waiting."

"Swerve!" yelled Zak.

Moon twisted the handlebars on the bike in the nick

of time. Bullets sprayed the road a fraction of a second after the bike went veering to one side.

"Hang on!" Moon shouted, wrenching the handlebars again and sending the bike slewing to the other side of the road.

Zak clung on to her grimly as he listened to the whine and skip of bullets. Then the firing stopped. He risked another look back – and wished he hadn't. The Range Rover was coming up fast. It was no more than twenty metres behind them now. He could see Milos's eyes flashing as he glared at them in red-faced fury. Giorgio was hammering a new clip into the machine pistol. Any second now and the deadly rain of bullets would begin again.

"Hold tight – I'm going in!" shouted Moon.

Zak hardly had a moment to wonder what she meant by *going in* when she sent the bike ploughing across the road again. But this time she didn't turn the handlebars at the last moment – this time she drove the bike right over the verge and into the trees.

Zak gritted his teeth and kept his head down as the bike careered through the forest, whipped by branches and clawed by thorns. They bumped and bounced, missing trees by millimetres, hurtling across sudden dips and almost toppling over when they hit roots and ridges.

Moon had crazy driving skills! Even at breakneck speed, she threaded her way safely through the forest. All the same, Zak let out a gasp of relief when the bike plunged out of the trees, all four wheels clear of the ground – and came crunching down in open land.

"That was fun!" Moon hollered. "Want to do it again?"

Zak was about to tell her she was nuts, when a low rumbling boom came shivering through the air from somewhere behind them.

Moon brought the bike to a spinning halt, facing back to the forest. A bloom of black cloud rose above the treetops, boiling upwards, lined with rolling red fire.

"That wasn't meant to happen," she said.

"What is it?" Zak asked as the pall of dark smoke rose higher.

"That's Eldorado going up in flames," said Moon. "I rigged a time-bomb in the armaments store. That was the insurance I mentioned. I was going to tell Milos about it if we got caught. I was going to tell him I'd only defuse it if he let you go."

Zak stared at her. "What about *you*?"

"I can handle myself," she said in a dismissive way that Zak found less than convincing. "I thought that you could zip off to the harbour and get away from this island double-quick." She shrugged. "Whatever they did to me, their set-up here would be blown." She frowned. "I put a ten-hour timer on the bomb – I don't get how it went up so soon."

"Did you booby-trap it?" asked Zak. "If Emil woke up and saw the time-bomb, he might have tried to defuse it."

Moonbeam nodded. "That has to be it," she said. "Poor Emil. Still, he wouldn't have known what hit him." She grimaced. "It's a shame the place went up, though. We probably lost some valuable intel. Hunter is not going to be pleased."

Shaking her head, she twisted the throttle and turned the bike away from the explosion. "No time for sight-seeing, Silver. Things to do, places to be. We need to get to the harbour before Milos and his pal do." The bike roared off again with Zak clinging onto Moon as if his life depended on it.

For a while, Zak's attention was concentrated on staying on the bike as it roared across the stony scrubland. He noticed that the land was gradually rising and becoming more rocky, heading towards the narrow high point he had seen on the map – the slender causeway that linked the two halves of Mad Cat Cay.

Moon steered the quad bike around a fist of bare rock and they came bouncing back onto the road as it rose towards the causeway. Zak only had a moment to be grateful before he heard the growl of Milos's Range Rover, no more than fifty metres behind them.

Now Moon really let rip, wrenching the throttle to its sticking point. They hurtled up the road at bone-jarring speed.

The road grew rapidly steeper, lined with rocks and knuckles of stone. They were on the causeway. Zak's eyes widened in alarm; the road was no more than five or six metres wide – and on either side the land fell away in steep rocky cliffs.

One wrong move . . . one slip of the fingers on the handlebars . . .

Gunfire rang out then stopped abruptly. Zak glanced back. The Range Rover had halved the distance between them, but Giorgio was wrestling with the machine pistol. Zak guessed it must have jammed. That was a blessing, at least – but it only postponed the inevitable. The speed at which the Range Rover was moving meant that it would catch them in a few seconds.

"Faster!" Zak shrieked into Moon's ear. "They're right behind us."

Moon flashed a look back, and her eyes were wild, her mouth stretched in a wind-blown grin, her red hair flying. She hit the brakes and the bike screeched to a halt.

"No!" howled Zak in a panic. "What are you . . . ?"

She spun the bike around, revved the engine and drove straight at the Range Rover.

Had she gone crazy? They'd be killed!

For a few terrifying moments the two vehicles drove straight at one another. Twenty metres apart. Ten. Five.

Zak saw Milos staring through the windscreen, his teeth gritted. Moon hunched over, piling on the speed. Reckless to the point of insanity.

At the very last moment, Milos spun the wheel to avoid the head-on collision. Moon tweaked the handle-bars and slammed on the brakes as the bike veered to the edge of the road.

Zak saw the Range Rover flash past, Milos fighting with the wheel, Giorgio stumbling and falling back. For a moment, it seemed as though Milos would regain control – but a front wheel dropped off the edge of the road, and the Range Rover dipped, tipping over. There was the scream of metal on stone, then the vehicle was gone.

Zak heard a dull, echoing crunch from way below.

The quad bike stood on the brink of the long fall, its engine growling.

Moon's face was grim and set. "Oops, sorry, Mr Milos," she said under her breath. "My fault!"

Zak stared at her, his mouth half open.

"What?" she said. "They were going to kill us, Silver."

"Yes, but . . ." He shook his head. He felt very disturbed that two people had just lost their lives because of them – even if those two people were terrorists. "Never mind," he murmured. She was right, he had to try and get used to this kind of thing. Milos and Giorgio had meant them nothing but harm – and they'd paid for it with their lives.

"Too right, *never mind*," Moon said, revving the engine and turning the bike around. "This job isn't always pretty, Silver."

She drove the bike to the far end of the causeway. The southern half of Mad Cat Cay fell away in front of them in a tumble of scrubland and barren rocks. The road wound down to the distant blue shimmer of the sea.

Zak could make out two arms of land, curling towards one another like claws. And in the bay between the claws, a small group of boats lay at harbour.

"There's our ride to the mainland," said Moon, revving as they accelerated down the long coil of the road. "There'll be a radio aboard for sure." She grinned over her shoulder. "We can call home – do you think they'll have missed us?"

Zak nodded. "I think they will," he said.

CHAPTER **THIRTEEN**

FORTRESS.
09:23 THURSDAY.
NINETEEN HOURS LATER.

Zak and Moon had managed a few hours of light sleep on the aeroplane back to London Heathrow, but as they sat in a Fortress briefing room with Colonel Hunter across the desk from them, Zak felt as if he hadn't had a real rest for a couple of months.

No sooner had they arrived at Fortress, after a hair-raising drive from the airport, than the Colonel had wanted a full report of everything that had happened since Flight P17 had gone off radar.

It took a while for Zak and Moon to tell him the entire story. He scribbled notes and asked sharp, pertinent questions every now and then.

"So, Milos is dead?" the Colonel asked.

"I should think so," Moon replied. "He went over a hundred-metre cliff straight into the sea. I can't imagine him living through that."

"And the villa was destroyed?" added Colonel Hunter.

"There was enough explosive there to demolish a football stadium," Moon said ruefully. "I don't think much would have survived."

"Pity," said the Colonel. "There would probably have been some useful information on Dr Avon's computer." He looked at Moonbeam. "I'm not questioning your judgment, agent. I think you did exactly the right thing in the circumstances. But we're still having difficulties accessing all the information on the laptop Dr Avon sent me."

"If both of the Burning Sky machines were destroyed in the explosion, the terrorist attack can't happen, can it?" said Zak. "Is it so urgent to get the info now?"

"We shouldn't assume everything has been destroyed," said the Colonel. "The FBI have sent their crack teams to

Mad Cat Cay, so if there's anything left, it will certainly be found. Perhaps you're right and we're in the clear – perhaps all that remains of Burning Sky is what's on Dr Avon's laptop. But I won't be easy in my mind until Bug gets that final folder open."

"I don't understand that," said Zak. "Surely Dr Avon wanted you to be able to get into the folder – that was the whole point of sending it to you. So why did he protect it with a totally unbreakable password?"

"Alexi knows the answer to that," said Moon. "Except apparently he *doesn't*. Silver's right – it doesn't make any sense."

"Alexi was exhausted when Switchblade brought him in mid-morning yesterday," said the Colonel. "I spoke to him briefly, but he was too tired for me to question him properly. We put him to bed for a few hours then I had Switchblade sit with him for a while." The Colonel shook his head wearily. "The boy told Switchblade everything that Dr Avon said to him, virtually word for word. I had it recorded and we've been analysing it ever since, trying every possible permutation of the words Dr Avon used, applying every code-breaking system we know – and still nothing."

"It'll be like one of those stupid riddles where the answer stares you right in the face the moment you solve it," said Moonbeam. "It has to be really simple – Dr Avon must have assumed it could be worked out in no time, once Alexi had told us everything that happened when they met."

"So, what's gone wrong?" asked Zak.

"What, indeed," said Colonel Hunter. "All we can hope is that something clicks in Alexi's mind, something so trivial he never thought to mention it."

"Is there any news on Dr Avon?" asked Zak, remembering the unmade bed in that little basement room.

"Nothing yet." The Colonel got up. "The two of you can stand down for the rest of the day. You've both done good work. I'm going to . . ."

The door crashed open. Bug stood there, breathing hard, his face twisted with anxiety. "I missed something," he gasped. "There was so much stuff in the folders that I didn't notice it." He gulped in breath. "It's a ghost file," he continued in a rush. "Hidden in among all the tech stuff. I've just decoded it. It says there were two versions of the Burning Sky device made."

"We already know that, Bug," said the Colonel. "Quick-silver saw photo images of them. They were in the villa – they would have been destroyed."

Bug's eyes bulged. "No," he gasped. "According to the info on the ghost file, only one of them was still on the island – the other one had been taken away by Milos's son. He was going to use it to demonstrate the weapon's destructive capabilities to Conquistador's potential buyers." He sucked in a deep breath. "It's *here*, Control!" he almost shouted. "Right here in London!"

Fortress was on high alert. Every available agent was in the main briefing room. Only Switchblade was missing – he was in another room with Alexi Roman, questioning him yet again, desperate to unravel the secret that Dr Avon had left with him. The secret that would reveal the full details of the terrorist attack Dr Avon had warned them about. If they could ever get it out of him.

The information they had so far was profoundly disturbing.

"We know Burning Sky is operational," the Colonel told them, striding the width of the room as he spoke, clearly agitated. "And we have good reason to believe it is in London, due to be unleashed some time between midnight tonight and midnight tomorrow."

Tomorrow was Friday – the day Milos had asked his clients to keep tuned to the international news media.

"From what we know of the device so far, it seems most likely that its target will be an aircraft," the Colonel continued. The information he was referring to had partly been taken from the folders Bug had opened, and partly from what Zak could remember of what he'd seen on the computer in Dr Avon's cell – especially that unnerving diagram of a plane being hit.

The Colonel pressed a button on a remote and the huge plasma screen at his back lit up with a map of the Greater London area. "Teams will be sent to the three major international airports," he said, sending a red arrow sliding across the screen. "Stansted in the north, Heathrow to the west and Gatwick to the south. You can all imagine, I'm sure, the devastation and loss of life that would follow the downing of an incoming passenger airliner at any of these airports. And for all we know about this device, they could just pick aeroplane after aeroplane out of the sky."

Zak shivered, imagining the horrible scene in his mind. Hundreds and hundreds of people could be killed.

"Wouldn't it be possible to divert all air traffic for the day, Control?" asked an agent.

"That wouldn't solve our problem, it would only delay it," said the Colonel. "If Conquistador's son sees that no planes are moving, he'll postpone the attack and reschedule it for another time and possibly another place. That's the last thing we want." He looked at the map, sliding the red arrow from place to place. "As well as the major airports, there is London City Airport, and several other air terminals in close proximity to London. Luton in the north, Southend Airport to the east, Oxford Airport, Biggin Hill and Ashford. There is also the Heliport on the South Bank of the Thames, although that's considered a less likely target."

So many possible targets. Project 17 would be spread very thin.

"I have issued an all-points Alpha Code alert," said the Colonel. "Every branch of MI5 and all the emergency services in the capital will be involved in the operation, which has the codename Firewall. During the course of this afternoon you will all have the details of your assignments downloaded onto your Mobs. You will co-operate fully with our colleagues in MI5, and do what you can to help the civilian authorities." His voice took on an even grimmer tone than usual. "I don't need to tell you how vital it is that you give this operation your absolute commitment."

Zak knocked on the door and waited.

The voice that responded was fragile and subdued. "Come in."

Zak opened the door and stepped into one of Project 17's spare sleeping rooms. This was the first chance he'd had to meet with Alexi since they'd parted backstage at Carnegie Hall – and that felt as though it had happened three lifetimes ago.

Alexi was sitting on the bed, his elbows on his knees, his shoulders hunched. He didn't look up as Zak entered.

"How's it going?" Zak asked, feeling suddenly awkward. Stupid question – from the look of Alexi, it wasn't going well at all. "Can I get you anything . . . or . . . ?" His voice trailed off as Alexi raised his head.

His eyes were red-rimmed and watery. He had obviously been crying. An unpleasant sensation struck Zak in the pit of his stomach. His mind writhed with a mix of embarrassment and sympathy and understanding.

Best to ignore it. He must be feeling bad because of not being able to figure out that *key* thing. Go on – be a friend – cheer the poor guy up.

"Haven't they even got you a piano?" Zak asked, trying to sound light-hearted. "Stingy bunch." He smiled hard. "Mind you, I'm not sure they could get one of those grand pianos in here – not unless they took the bed out and you slept on top of it."

Alexi looked up at him with empty eyes. "Dr Avon is dead," he murmured. "Switchblade told me. The news just came through from America. They found his . . . body . . . buried under leaves in Miami – in a place called

Coral Reef Park."

Zak's mind went into free-fall. He saw again that sad basement room. He saw Dr Avon's terrified face on the plasma screen in the briefing room. He heard his voice.

"I'm really sorry," he said. "That's horrible." He couldn't think what else to say. Alexi dropped his face into his hands. Zak hesitated, thinking maybe he should just leave.

Instead, he sat down on the side of the bed next to Alexi.

"Switchblade said they just left him there like that because he didn't matter to them any more," mumbled Alexi. "Once they'd got his secrets from him . . . they just . . . threw him away . . ."

"That's bad," Zak said softly. Alexi didn't respond.

Zak didn't say anything more. He just sat quietly beside Alexi, staring at his own shoes.

Zak wasn't sure how much time went by before the door opened quietly and Colonel Hunter came into the room.

He crouched in front of Alexi, resting a hand on his shoulder. "I'm very sorry," he said. "I can arrange to put a call through to your grandmother. Would you like to speak to her?"

Alexi nodded.

Colonel Hunter stood up again. "I'll get that organized straight away," he said. "Alexi, look at me." His voice was firm but gentle. "I don't want you to worry about anything," he said. "I want you to rest – get some sleep if you can. I promise you the moment we know everything is safe, we'll get you home."

"Thank you," said Alexi.

Colonel Hunter moved to the door. "Can I borrow Quicksilver for a few moments, Alexi?" he asked.

Alexi nodded, looking up at Zak. "Thanks," he said.

Zak followed Colonel Hunter into the corridor. The Colonel closed the door very quietly.

"Bug tells me your replacement Mob is ready," he said. "Go and fetch it – it'll have your Firewall assignment downloaded onto it by now." He frowned. "You should get some sleep too – you look exhausted. I'll ask someone else to sit with Alexi." He nodded. "It was good of you, staying with him like that."

Zak gave a bleak smile. He wasn't sure he'd done anything at all.

He made his way to Bug's office.

"Have you heard about Dr Avon?" asked Bug as he entered.

Zak nodded, not wanting to talk about it. "Control says you've sorted my Mob for me," he said.

Bug reached forward and picked up a Mob from his workstation. "It's got everything on it from your original," he said.

"Thanks." With a brief nod, Zak walked out. He really didn't feel like chatting to anyone right then. He just wanted to be on his own for a while.

He walked to his room, quickly scrolling through his replacement Mob, checking nothing was missing. Every Mob was permanently linked to the networked computers in Bug's office, sending constant streams of data back and forth so that the exact location of every field agent could be followed in real time, and any information they put on their Mob would be instantly downloaded at Fortress.

He saw an incoming message.

Operation Firewall. Agent Quicksilver's Assignment. London City Airport. 22:00 to 06.00 shift.

His heart sank. He hadn't been assigned one of the major airports – and he would be up all night.

Zak kicked his shoes off and threw himself onto his bed. He flicked the screen to bring up the recording he had made of Alexi in New York. He played it, laying the Mob on the pillow beside his head, closing his eyes to listen again.

He was asleep in minutes.

CHAPTER **FOURTEEN**

Two men in blue overalls were busy in an unoccupied flat near the top of a tall, newly built apartment building near the South Bank of the River Thames. One had thick, dark hair and skin tanned a leathery brown, the other was pale with fine hair and eyes almost as clear as glass.

The pale-eyed man was on the balcony of the apartment, using a cordless electric drill to anchor a metal cradle to the outer wall. The other was inside the empty and unfurnished living room, squatting on the floor next to a pair of large holdalls, tapping the keyboard of a laptop computer.

One of the holdalls contained the second prototype of Burning Sky.

The name of the dark-haired man was Pavlos Milos. A silent rage burned inside him as he worked. He had learned through his international contacts about the fireball that had engulfed his father's villa on Mad Cat Cay. He did not know who had been responsible for his father's death – the man had many enemies. That was natural in his line of work. Pavlos hoped that the British had been involved – British Security had certainly been active on some level with all the trouble caused by Emil and Giorgio when they had been so stupid as to let the scientist escape.

He hoped British Security had been responsible for the explosion, because it would make what was going to happen tomorrow all the more satisfying.

As Spyros Milos's eldest son, Pavlos would have inherited his father's business, but now, with Mad Cat Cay swarming with FBI agents, he would have to find a new base from which to work – he would need to start almost from scratch.

But he did have one advantage. He had control of Burning Sky.

The demonstration of the EMP device would go ahead as planned. A fitting epitaph for his father. And a fine way to announce his own presence on the world stage. Spyros Milos may be dead, but the codename Conquistador would outlive him – in the form of his twenty-one-year-old son.

The pale man came in from the balcony.

"It is ready," he mumbled in a thick Russian accent.

"Good," Pavlos responded. "My work is also nearly complete."

The man irritated Pavlos with his stupidity. But he was a useful creature to have at one's side. Trained by the FSB, the Russian Security Service, he was a formidable fighting machine. If by some mischance they were discovered early, Boris would stop anyone from getting to Burning Sky before it could be activated.

Pavlos typed in a final clearance code and stood up. He looked at his watch. Once Burning Sky was in place in its cradle and precision-aimed at its target, they would be ready to rock and roll. Pavlos grinned savagely. But he would wait until the time his father had chosen.

They would stay here. Eat a little. Sleep, maybe. And tomorrow morning the unsuspecting people of London would discover first hand the awesome power of Burning Sky.

It would be a lesson they would not quickly forget!

✳

Zak had set the alarm of his Mob to wake him at 20:30. That would give him plenty of time to shower and grab a bite to eat and generally get his head together before his overnight shift at the small Thames-side London City Airport. It was a single-runway airport that was only capable of handling medium-sized passenger aircraft, and as far as Zak was concerned, staking it out was a waste of time and resources. As if anyone would bother using a weapon like Burning Sky to take down a plane with only about fifty people on board.

He awoke with a start a full half hour before the alarm sounded.

A strange dream had shocked him out of sleep. He had been on The Run – the punishing physical course that every British Intelligence agent had to undergo as part of their basic training. It involved making your way to a specific target in a specially constructed townscape, while being pursued by enemies whose only interest was in taking you down hard and fast.

Zak had done well on The Run, but afterwards he had been told that a single agent had once done better. An agent codenamed Slingshot. His mother had been an MI5 agent. Had she been Slingshot? According to Colonel Hunter, no. But Zak had the strong feeling that the Colonel wasn't telling him the whole truth.

The identity of Slingshot was still a mystery that niggled at Zak like an itch he couldn't scratch.

Hence the dream, he assumed.

Because in the dream, he was absolutely certain that he was chasing Slingshot through the fake town. The fleeting figure in front of him had been dressed all in black, a black ski mask hiding the face. Slingshot had always been at least one step ahead of Zak, right up to the end, when they'd both gone crashing through the doors of the target building.

Zak had thrown himself forwards, and he'd brought Slingshot down in a spectacular rugby tackle. He'd heaved the struggling agent over and ripped off the mask.

The face staring up at him had been his own face.

He'd woken up with the shock of it.

Weird.

Weird and unsettling.

But he was awake now. Wide awake.

He showered and dressed. There was some time to kill before he needed to be at the airport. He went to check on Alexi. He knocked softly on the door and opened it a crack. The room beyond was in darkness. He could hear soft snoring.

Alexi was asleep.

That was good, the poor guy needed to be out of it for a while, after everything he'd been through recently.

Zak closed the door again and headed to Bug's office. Officially, Bug only worked a few hours a day around his schooling, but because Bug's hobby was also his work, he could often be found in his office in the evening, wrestling with some computer problem, or inventing new Mob apps just for the fun of it.

Sure enough, Bug was in there – in his default position, folded up in his executive chair with his feet on the workstation top and the keyboard on his knees.

The eight plasma screens were running some kind of program – columns and columns of numbers and letters were flashing on all the screens, changing more rapidly than Zak could follow. He guessed Bug was still searching for the key to that final folder.

Then Zak noticed that Bug's head was hanging forwards and his hands were dangling over the arms of the chair. Bug had dozed off. Zak crept forwards, meaning to give Bug a poke in the ribs to wake him with a start.

He stopped. A tablet computer lay in Bug's lap. Zak leaned closer, his eyes widening.

The screen was displaying a pale blue page.

SECURITY SERVICES – MI5

ALPHA CLEARANCE FILES. EYES ONLY.

NO HARD COPIES.

Below the title, was a search box.

In it, Bug had typed **SLINGSHOT.**

Some time ago Zak had asked Bug to try and find out anything he could about the agent called Slingshot, but Colonel Hunter had given Bug a hard time about making unauthorized searches, and as far as Zak was aware, Bug had stopped looking.

Or maybe not . . . ?

Zak knew that Bug had worked on the Slingshot problem for fun – enjoying the challenge of hacking into codeword-protected files. Maybe he was still trying to solve the puzzle for his own entertainment?

Zak read down the page.

SEARCH RESULTS.

Searched for Slingshot. Result 1.

Search took 0.09 seconds.

MI5 agent Slingshot.

Real Name: JASON TRENT. AKA JASON WYNDHAM.

Authorization Code: ALPHA-LOCKED

FILE. MINISTERIAL CLEARANCE NEEDED.

Bug's fingers twitched and his head lifted with a jerk. He stared up at Zak, blinking rapidly.

"What's that?" Zak asked, pointing at the computer screen in his lap.

Bug was flustered. He looked around Zak towards the door, as though afraid someone else might be there. "You shouldn't creep up on me like that." There was a hint of annoyance in his voice. "You frightened the life out of me!"

"I thought you'd stopped chasing Slingshot," said Zak.

"I had," said Bug. "This is just . . ." He paused. "I sometimes do some searching between other things – just for fun, you know?" He gestured to the plasma screens where the columns of numbers and letters were still changing at mind-boggling speed. "I can't do anything else to try and get Dr Avon's folder open till that's finished running. " His eyes gazed out from under his heavy fringe. "I was using the time to work on the Slingshot problem." His voice dropped to a whisper. "I'm looking into ways of sidestepping the usual proto-cols. Control will thank me if I discover holes in the security network." He frowned. "You shouldn't have seen this," he added, nodding at the screen. "I had to come up with some pretty complicated stuff to sneak in *this* far."

"My parents' names were John and Janet Trent," Zak said slowly. "So, who's *Jason* Trent? And what's with the AKA Jason Wyndham thing?"

"I don't know," said Bug. "I've been stuck on this page for days. Ministerial Clearance Codes are a total nightmare to break. You have to be really careful, or the whole house comes crashing down on you."

A chime rang out from the eight screens. The flickering columns had come to a halt. On each screen was displayed the same wording.

Quantum Cryptanalysis results: 0

"Oh, *no!*" groaned Bug, flicking a finger over the tablet computer screen to close the page. He grabbed his keyboard and began typing. "I was sure that would work," he muttered. "I've tried everything – the Kasiski examination, brute force attack, Shor and Grover's algorithms, a rainbow table, integral and linear methods – even elliptic curve protocols. Everything! What *is* it with this code?"

Zak was desperate to find out more about the man called Jason Trent, AKA Jason Wyndham. Were they aliases used by his father? Was *he* Slingshot? Was that the secret Colonel Hunter was keeping from him – that both his mother and father were MI5 agents?

But why would Colonel Hunter reveal his mother was in MI5 but conceal the fact that his father was as well? There didn't seem much point in that, unless there was something about his father that *had* to be kept from him? Bug needed to dig deeper.

Zak knew this was no time for mysteries. Bug needed all his computer savvy to break that code and find out about the terrorist attack – otherwise people were going to die.

Zak glanced at his Mob. 21:05. It was time for him to go to the assembly point for the journey to London City Airport.

Zak sat in a small, grey room. Bored and frustrated. Two men were sitting close by at a wide desk, drinking frequent cups of coffee and staring at a wide array of grainy CCTV screens. This was the security centre of London City Airport. The entire airport was criss-crossed with surveillance cameras, inside and out.

The place was very quiet and most of the screens were so empty of action they could have been photographs. Occasionally, a member of ground staff would wander past, or a police officer or plain-clothed MI5 agent on the prowl, the cameras picking them up in sequence as they made their way from one area to another, but on the whole, the airport was dead.

Zak sighed. Hardly surprising. The last flight in had been from Zurich – it had landed at 21:05 – almost an hour before Zak arrived. The first flight due in wouldn't arrive till 07:55. There were no departures between nine at night and eight in the morning either.

He looked at his Mob. 03:47. He yawned.

At least at the major airports like Heathrow, things would be gearing up for the first flight in soon. Nothing was going to happen here for hours – and by the time the action started cranking up at London City, his shift would be over and he'd be back in Fortress going beddy-byes for the Colonel.

Irritating and frustrating.

He flicked a finger across his Mob and opened a channel to listen in on Project 17 chatter from Heathrow. Icewater and Dragonfire had been sent there, the lucky pair. The chat was all: *Terminal 5 checked, it's clean, Ice, I'm heading over to Terminal 4 now. Roger that, Dragon, it's all quiet in Terminal 1, as well. Keep me posted.*

Windtalker and Jackhammer were at Gatwick. Wildcat and Moonbeam had been sent to Stansted. In fact, almost everyone else was somewhere interesting. And here he was, doing nothing useful and trying not to doze off.

Things were beginning to liven up at London City Airport. Ground staff were starting to arrive, and a few early-bird passengers were queuing to check in. The airport was gradually coming alive.

Zak was tuned in on MI5 and police frequencies on his Mob, listening to the brief reports as the minutes ticked past. All luggage was being thoroughly checked, and the hand-luggage x-ray and the metal detecting portals were ready to start screening people and their possessions.

Zak's Mob played the bouncy tune he'd programmed to let him know Switchblade was calling. It was 05:50.

"Okay, Silver," came Switch's voice. "I've just arrived. You can go now."

Fantastic! The minute things start to get interesting, he was being sent back to Fortress. Absolutely brilliant!

"I can stay on, if you like," Zak suggested.

"You've just done eight hours," came Switchblade's voice. "You need some sleep. Control will probably want you out again for the 14:00 shift, if nothing happens before then. Get back to Fortress. I'm taking over now."

With a deep sigh, Zak pocketed his Mob and made for the door.

He came out into the cool early morning air. At one of the airports near here, some crazy people were planning to bring down an aeroplane full of innocent passengers. He remembered the terror and panic he'd felt as the Lear jet had gone down. Imagine that times a couple of hundred!

He screwed his hands into fists. "I can't just go to bed," he muttered. "Control's got to be kidding if he thinks that's going to work."

He walked to the taxi rank. He had a smart card in his pocket to pay the fare.

"Moorgate station, please," he said, getting in. The quickest way to access Fortress was via a secret entrance near Moorgate underground station.

He sat back, fuming quietly as the taxi cruised away from the airport and headed west.

He was so not sleepy.

A sudden thought struck him. He leaned forwards. "Can you make that Waterloo station, please?"

He'd go and pay a visit to Dodge. It felt like an age since they'd met up – and Dodge was the one person he could talk to and know anything he said would go no further.

*

The sun was just starting to rise in the sky as Zak and Dodge sat on a bench in Jubilee Gardens. The London Eye towered above them as they sat under the trees, gazing out over the River Thames and eating hotdogs.

Zak knew better than to talk about Operation Firewall with his friend. It would be an appalling breach of protocol for him to let slip anything about an on-going operation – even to someone he trusted with his life.

"Sorry I haven't been around for so long, Dodge," said Zak through a mouthful of hotdog. "My life's been crazy busy recently."

Dodge smiled and nodded. "Friendship should be more than biting time can sever, Zachary," he replied in his deep, growling voice. "And forgiveness is the oil of relationships."

"Is it?" Zak said with a crooked grin. "That's good to know." He liked Dodge's quotes, even though he didn't understand half of them.

Dodge hadn't altered a bit since Zak had last seen him. He still wore that crumpled and frayed old pin-striped suit, and those boots held together by duct tape. Half of his lean, hawk-like face was hidden behind a thick brown beard, and his bushy eyebrows stuck out wildly above his keen, dark eyes. During the warmer months, he slept rough in various little boltholes around the city, but he could usually be found in a shelter he called The Mansion – a tiny hut made of hardboard under the arches of Waterloo Station.

Dodge never talked about his past, and Zak knew better than to ask him, although he had often wondered how someone as smart and savvy as Dodge had ended up with nothing except the clothes he stood up in.

He imagined some tragedy or catastrophe lay somewhere in Dodge's secret past.

"A hotdog goes down well for breakfast," said Dodge. "You're a good lad, Zachary."

Zak looked at him sideways. "How are you doing, Dodge?" he asked.

"Can't complain," said Dodge, scrunching up the hotdog wrapper and launching it at a nearby bin. "I have fine food, fine company and the sun on my face. Life's good today, Zachary. Very good."

"I've found out some stuff about my parents," said Zak all of a sudden, the need to unburden himself bursting out of him in a rush.

"Tell me about them, if you'd like to," said Dodge.

He listened with silent attention while Zak explained all that he had learned about his dead mother and father, as well as what little he knew of the mysterious agent codenamed Slingshot.

"And there's something else," Zak said hesitantly. "Bug has found a file showing that Slingshot's real name is either Jason Trent or Jason Wyndham." He looked urgently at his friend. "Trent is my parents' last name," he added. "What do you make of that, Dodge?"

Dodge's heavy brows knitted together. "You say your father's first name was James – but could Jason have been an alias, do you think?" he said.

Zak nodded. "That's exactly what I was wondering," he replied. "But why would Colonel Hunter tell me that my mother was an MI5 agent, then hide the fact that my father was as well? It doesn't make sense." He frowned. "Does it?"

Dodge shook his shaggy head. "It doesn't seem to," he said. "But I have a possible solution to your problem."

Zak's eyes lit up. "What?" he breathed.

"Ask Colonel Hunter," said Dodge. "Tell him you need to know the full facts."

"That's going to get Bug into trouble," said Zak.

"Not if you tell the truth," said Dodge. "Bug was checking the files for possible hacking loopholes and you saw them by accident."

"Oh. Yes. That's exactly how it happened." Of course – going to the Colonel *was* the obvious thing to do.

Switchblade's bouncing melody sounded from Zak's Mob. It was in his pocket. Zak let it go to voicemail. If anything significant had happened, Control would be in touch. Switch was probably just checking whether Zak was in bed yet.

Dodge gazed at Zak, his eyebrows raised. "You're not going to answer it?" he asked.

"No, it's only Switch," said Zak.

"How do you know that without even looking?" asked Dodge.

Zak sometimes forgot how out of touch with modern technology his friend could be. "Everyone on my Mob has a dedicated ringtone," he explained. "That one's for Switch, Bug's tone is a croaking frog – and so on."

Dodge shook his head. "The marvels of the modern age," he said. "Different melodies that give you different information." He sighed. "How science and technology multiply around us!"

Zak smiled. "It's all pretty normal stuff these days . . ." His voice trailed away. Dodge's words echoed in his mind.

Different melodies that give you different information . . .

Something clicked. Something astounding!

Zak let out a yell as he yanked his Mob out of his pocket. It was as if a door had opened in his skull and sunlight had come flooding into his brain.

Fumbling a little, he accessed the recording he had made of Alexi Roman that first time they had met in the Graves Apartment in New York. He turned the volume up full, listening intently – but not to Alexi's voice. He was listening to the tinkling single-note melody Alexi was playing on the piano as he spoke. The melody that he said Dr Avon had played to him.

Could it be that simple? Top brains had been working on this code non-stop – was it really possible that *he* had solved it? Had he come up with an idea that no one else had even considered?

Dodge was watching him carefully. "You've had a revelation, Zachary?" he asked.

"Yes. Maybe. Possibly," said Zak, babbling. "I'm not sure."

What had Moon said? That it would be something really simple. But *this* simple?

With trembling fingers and a pounding heart, Zak pressed Bug's access code.

"Hi," came Bug's slightly sleepy voice. "It's only half past seven. What's up?"

"Are you in the tech room?" gabbled Zak.

"Yes, I'm trying out some more decryption stuff," Bug replied. "I was just . . ."

"Can you get at the recording I made of Alexi?" Zak interrupted him. "The one on my Mob."

"Sure, I can," said Bug. "What of it? I've got half a dozen different recordings of what he told us."

"Not with piano accompaniment, you haven't!" cried Zak.

Bug's voice was puzzled. "What are you talking about?"

"Dr Avon played a tune to Alexi – on the piano," said Zak, almost shouting down the Mob. "Alexi played it to me when I was talking to him. I think the key to getting that last file open might be in that piece of music! What if it was never numbers or letters at all – what if it was musical notes?"

"Hold on," came Bug's voice again, suddenly sharp and fully alert. "I'm accessing the voicepod file. Okay, I'm there. I'm listening to it."

Come on! Come on!

"Yes, I hear the piano," muttered Bug. "I'm clipping the pod at both ends so I can work on it more easily. Okay, I'm going to put it through some filters to take the voices and other extraneous noises out."

Zak pressed his Mob so hard against his head that it hurt his ear – not that he cared. Faintly, he heard the tinkle of the piano notes.

"I just need to clean it up a bit more," mumbled Bug. "Okay, that's good. That should work. Now, I'm going to patch the pod into the last file from Dr Avon's laptop."

"And?" Zak almost screamed. "Is it working?"

"Hold on," muttered Bug. "No. Nothing so far . . ."

Zak's heart sank. He'd been so sure.

"It's working!" came Bug's astonished voice. "I can't believe it!" He let out a whoop. "Silver! You total genius! The file's open. I'm looking at it! I'm looking at it right now!"

CHAPTER **FIFTEEN**

Colonel Hunter had been up all night, prowling the large Fortress ops room, coordinating Project 17's involvement in Operation Firewall. He was on a conference call with the Director General of MI5, the Commissioner of the Metropolitan Police and the Home Secretary when the call from Bug came.

Less than a minute later, he was in Bug's office, his fingers gripping the back of Bug's chair as he stared at a video of his old friend Stephen Avon.

Dr Avon looked tired and pale, but there was a fierce light burning in his eyes. He was leaning into the webcam, speaking in a low, rapid voice.

"I knew you'd work out how to open the file, Peter," he said. "You were always good at thinking outside the box." His eyes flickered nervously. "Listen to me, Peter, I'm going to make an escape bid tonight. If I fail, you'll never see this, but I have to try – whatever they do to me."

Bug glanced up at the Colonel's face. The only outward sign of what he was thinking came from a narrowing of his eyes and a slight twitch of his jaw.

"I'm being held on an island called Mad Cat Cay, just north of the Bahamas. I can't give you exact coordinates, but I know it's about one hundred kilometres due east of mainland Florida, of Miami."

"We know this, Stephen," Colonel Hunter growled under his breath. "Tell us what we need to know about the *attack.*"

"I'm being held by a man called Milos – he's forced me to finish my work on Burning Sky." Steven Avon's eyes were frantic. "I've constructed two of the devices for him – he plans to sell them on the international market to the highest bidder. That mustn't happen, Peter. The thing is absolutely deadly." Dr Avon wiped the sweat from his forehead and continued, his voice shaking. "Milos is sending his son to London to organize an attack with the weapon. I think I have one shot at preventing a disaster. I can't sabotage the weapon; Milos's son is too computer-savvy for me to get away with that. But I've included a GPS microchip in both of the machines. They can be tracked using a dedicated system I've set up on this laptop – in this folder."

"Have you found what he's talking about, Bug?" snapped the Colonel.

"Looking now, Control," muttered Bug, typing rapidly.

"I've just heard on the radio that Alexi Roman is in Miami," Dr Avon continued. "I'm going to break out of here as soon as it's dark. There are motorboats in the harbour on the south island. I'm going to make for it and do my best to get to Alexi. I'll play him the musical key, but I won't explain what it is. It's too dangerous for him to know about Burning Sky. Then I'm going to send you this laptop." Dr Avon's eyes were gleaming. "I'm sorry I had to make this so complex – but I couldn't risk anyone tracking down the parcel and being able to open this file. The information in here must never be made public – I'm relying on you to make sure of that. I trust no one, Peter, no one but you. Everything you need to stop the attack is in this file – but you need to do more, Peter, you need to make sure Burning Sky is *never* used. *Never!*"

Dr Avon reached forwards and the recording came to an abrupt end.

"Bug?" growled the Colonel. "The other file?"

"Got it, Control," said Bug. A new file opened on screen. A pinpoint-sharp satellite picture of a sprawling urban centre with a river winding through it. Bug typed and the picture zoomed in. A blue dot pulsed at the centre of the image, and from one side a narrow blue cone was being emitted, like the beam of light from a torch.

"It's London," Bug murmured, his eyes bulging. "Central London. The South Bank of the Thames." The image expanded rapidly. "I don't get it," muttered Bug as the blue light with its widening cone pulsed and the building complexes rushed towards them. "There aren't any airports near there."

"No, there aren't," growled Colonel Hunter. He leaned forwards and stabbed a finger against the plasma screen. "But there's *that*! And the weapon's beam is aimed straight at it!"

"What's going on?" Zak shouted into his Mob. He was walking backwards and forwards in front of the bench, unable to keep still. It was driving him crazy that he couldn't see what was happening in Bug's office. All he could hear were the voices. Dr Avon's recorded voice, and intermittent comments from Bug and Control.

Dodge was leaning forwards on the bench, watching him closely but saying nothing.

"Bug!" Zak yelled. "Talk to me!"

"Quicksilver?" It was Colonel Hunter's voice.

"Yes, I'm here."

"The target is Waterloo railway station," snapped the Colonel. "Dr Avon's GPS tracker system has located the Burning Sky weapon in a high rise apartment block overlooking the station. It's right on top of you, Quicksilver. Bug is patching the file through to you now. Burning Sky will show as a blue pulse."

A sharp ping sounded as the file arrived on Zak's Mob.

Zak jabbed the screen of his Mob to bring up the file. For a moment Zak didn't get it at all. It was as if he was looking at a picture brought up by the Mob's camera. Dodge was on-screen, sitting watching him from the bench.

But then the picture changed into the weirdest thing Zak had ever seen. The world he could see through the Mob was like an x-ray. Dodge was still sitting there, but he'd been reduced to strange, coloured outlines – and the bench was visible through him.

Amazed, Zak lifted the Mob and the screen revealed x-ray buildings, one superimposed on another. And through the buildings he could see traffic moving on the roads, and people bustling along the pavements.

"Unreal . . ." he murmured, roving the Mob and watching the bizarre scenery changing as if it was a living diagram. Through the immediate buildings and across the road, Zak could see the huge expanse of Waterloo station. People were moving about. He could see crowded escalators through the transparent walls. He saw trains. People jostling along platforms as the morning rush hour reached its height. He could even make out the shapes of buildings *behind* the station.

There was so much going on – so many layers of activity, that Zak could hardly take it all in. It was information overload.

And then he saw it!

Above and behind the station complex he could make out a tall building – with a blue pulse coming from somewhere close to the top.

"I have it!" he yelled into his Mob. "But I don't get it – how can an EMP hurt a train?"

"An electro-magnetic pulse would knock out all the electrics in and around the station," barked Colonel Hunter. "The signal lights would fail, the points would be locked, communication with the trains would be lost. Waterloo is Britain's busiest rail station – do you have any idea how many trains come and go in the rush hour? There will be absolute chaos, Quicksilver – can you imagine the loss of life that would occur if two or three high-speed commuter trains crashed into one another?"

Hundreds of people could be killed and injured. It would be an utter disaster.

"I'm putting out an alert," barked the Colonel. "There will be people with you very soon. If the weapon is going to be used in the morning rush hour, it might be triggered at any moment."

"Tell them to meet me there!" exclaimed Zak. He was already running, speeding across the wide grassy expanse of Jubilee Gardens, making for York Road and the busy station beyond.

He heard heavy feet close behind. He glanced around; Dodge was pounding along behind him.

"No, Dodge!" he called back. "You won't be able to keep up with me! Get away from here – I have to stop something really bad from happening!"

"I can help," Dodge shouted.

Zak didn't have time to worry about Dodge – he'd soon outrun him anyway. Except that he didn't.

It was partly the heavy traffic streaming along York Road, and partly the log-jam of early-morning commuters blocking the pavements, but Zak couldn't get into his running zone.

He constantly had to dive left and right to avoid people, and every time he looked back, Dodge was still only a few steps behind, and running well. Surprisingly well.

Zak checked his Mob. The blue beam was pulsing regularly from the building on the far side of the station. He hesitated, staring both ways along York Road, trying to work out which way to go.

He felt a hand on his shoulder. Dodge was right behind him, gazing down at the Mob, his eyes glittering with a sharpness that Zak had never seen before. "Follow me, Zachary," he said. "I know how to get there."

"But . . ."

Dodge didn't wait. He darted to the right along the crowded pavement.

There were too many people, and all of them in a mad rush to get where they were going. It was impossible to get through quickly. Burning Sky could be triggered at any moment, and they were stuck here. It was hopeless.

Suddenly, Dodge let out a shout, leaping to and fro and waving his arms and shrieking in a cracked high-pitched voice. "The foul fiend! The foul fiend bites my back!" People backed away with startled and alarmed looks, bumping into one another and leaving a wide pathway as he ran forwards, gesticulating and throwing his legs up and shouting. "Tom's a-cold! Bless thee from whirlwinds, star-blasting, and taking!"

If the situation hadn't been so deadly, Zak could almost have smiled at the way people were jostling and pushing at one another to give this ragged madman a clear path along the pavement.

He followed in Dodge's wake, keeping one eye on his Mob, dreading at any moment seeing the screen go blank, seeing the lights go out in the shops along York Road, seeing everything electrical die in an instant.

How long did they have? Minutes? Seconds?

At last, they came to a small side street that darted away under the high arch of the railway lines. There were far fewer people here, and Dodge was able to stop his crazy performance and concentrate on running. Graffiti and colourful murals decorated the walls of the tunnel, catching Zak's eye as he raced along at Dodge's side.

He was fast, Zak had to admit it. He would never have expected his friend to be able to move so quickly. But there was no time now to wonder about it as they came bursting out of the long tunnel and raced across the road, making for the tall apartment block that overlooked the station.

They crashed through the building's double glass doors. There was a plush carpet, modern paintings on the walls – and there was a bank of four lifts.

Dodge slammed his hand on the call button. A yellow arrow lit up, and the next moment the doors of one of the lifts slid silently open.

"Dodge, this is too dangerous," Zak began, but Dodge just shoved him into the lift.

"Which floor?" Dodge snapped. "Can you tell from your Mob?"

Zak held the Mob upwards, staring at the weird x-ray plan of the building. The blue beam seemed to be coming from the uppermost level. "The top!" Zak said. "When we get there, you keep right back!" Dodge hammered the button for the sixteenth floor. The doors hissed closed and the lift began to rise.

"Dodge?" Zak said urgently, tugging on his friend's sleeve. "Are you listening to me? You can't help me with this. I've been trained – you know I have. I know what to do." He wasn't at all sure he *did* know what to do – but he was certain of one thing: he didn't want Dodge coming to any harm.

Dodge looked at him, and there was the strangest light in his eyes. "Don't worry about me, Zachary," he said. "I was in the armed forces for eleven years."

Zak blinked at him. "You were a soldier?"

"I was," said Dodge.

Zak didn't know what to say. A thousand questions rattled through his brain. A *soldier?* Then how . . . why . . . what *happened?*

No time for that! Concentrate! Focus! Burning Sky! That's all you can think about right now.

The lift halted and the doors slid open.

Control's voice sounded from Zak's Mob. "Back-up is on the way, Quicksilver. Bug has just opened another file in the folder. The attack is planned to take place at zero-eight-hundred hours. Do you copy that?"

Zak looked at the time display on his Mob.

07:58.

His stomach turned over.

They only had two minutes.

They rushed out into a long carpeted hallway studded with numbered doors.

Dodge's eyes narrowed. "Zachary?"

Zak stared at the x-ray map, turning slowly until the screen flared with a throbbing blue light. He pointed. "This way!"

They came to a door. The screen of Zak's Mob was one blazing blue light now. It was so bright that he couldn't see anything through it any more.

They had ninety seconds.

Dodge drew back to the far side of the hallway then rushed at the door with his shoulder. It burst open. A short hall. Doors off. An open door at the end.

Zak ran into the room. It was completely empty. There wasn't even a carpet. He spun to the left – an archway led to another room, also bare, but not empty. Not empty at all.

A dark-haired man was kneeling on the floor at a laptop computer, his body tense. He turned towards Zak, an angry, startled look on his face.

"Boris!" he shouted, turning back to the keyboard and typing rapidly.

A big, beefy blond-haired man with pale eyes stepped into the archway. Without hesitating, Zak ran at him, hours of martial-arts unarmed-combat training whirling in his head.

Zak flung himself at the man, one leg rising high, his hips pivoting, his body revolving on the ball of one foot. He'd bring the man down with a wing chun round-house kick to his thigh. He'd been taught that a properly delivered kick had the same effect as hitting someone with a baseball bat. The man would drop to his knees with the pain – and then a second roundhouse to his head would finish the job.

But the man's own leg scythed across, almost quicker than Zak could follow, catching Zak's shin in mid-air, twisting him, wrenching his ankle and knee. He lurched backwards, his balance gone. The man's foot came out like a piston, striking him in the chest and sending him crashing headlong into the wall.

Dazed and in pain, hardly able to draw breath, Zak sprawled on the floor, his ears ringing, his chest burning. He saw Dodge leap forwards. He saw the pale-eyed man engage with him. He saw the two of them kicking and punching as they surged back and forth across the floor.

Dodge was giving him time – time to get to the device.

A few precious seconds.

He staggered to his feet and flung himself through the archway. Gathering himself, he ran at the other man. With a snarling smile, the man jabbed a finger down on the keyboard.

"Too late!" he shouted. "It's done!" He stood up, drawing a long serrated knife from his belt and moving to stand between Zak and the laptop.

Zak saw electric cables leading to an open balcony door. He jinked aside, narrowly avoiding the swinging knife. He flung himself onto the balcony. The Burning Sky device was there, anchored to the wall.

The device was humming, glowing with a cold white light, the power building rapidly towards its devastating climax.

Zak hurled himself at it, snatching the cables that fed into its rear panel. He swung on them, but they didn't come loose. Gasping in frustration he saw that the cables were attached with screws.

No time!

He grabbed the device and hauled at it with all his strength. For a moment it didn't move, but then Zak felt a strange giddying surge of power coursing through his arms. He heaved back, hearing the device being wrenched from the wall. He stumbled to the parapet of the balcony and flung the device off with all the force he could muster.

The cables fed down over the edge of the balcony as the device plummeted to the ground. It struck against one of the lower balconies and Zak saw it break into tumbling and spinning pieces. He heard the knife-man give a scream of rage. He half-turned, but all the strength seemed to have drained out of him; his legs buckled under him and he slid to the floor, his eyes swimming.

The man lunged at him, the knife held high. Zak threw his arms over his head, unable to get up – unable to do anything to save himself.

CHAPTER **SIXTEEN**

The knife blow never fell.

Zak heard a cry, cut short. The crash of a body hitting the floor. He dropped his arms, forcing his eyes to focus.

Dodge was crouching in front of him, his expression anxious.

"Zachary? Are you okay?"

"Did I do it in time?" Zak gasped, trying to get up. Why did he feel so weak?

"You did, Zachary," said Dodge, helping him to his feet and turning him so he could look over the balcony. He could see the wide expanse of the glass and steel roofs of Waterloo station stretched out below them. Multiple railway tracks fed out to the south-west. Trains were gliding smoothly along. Traffic was moving on the streets.

It was two minutes past eight in the morning, and everything was normal.

"You've injured yourself, Zachary," Dodge said, concerned.

Zak lifted his hands. There were cuts in his palms and fingers. There was blood and pain. "I had to rip the thing off the wall," he gasped.

Dodge frowned. "Judging by the holes left in the brickwork, it was anchored on there by half a dozen ten-millimetre coachbolts," said Dodge, his voice half-puzzled and half-amazed. "I couldn't have got it loose with a crowbar, never mind my bare hands!"

Zak gave a weak grin. "Just call me Superman." The weakness was beginning to ebb now and he found he could stand unaided. He remembered that sudden surge of power in his arms and across his chest; power that had helped him to pull the device off the wall, even though it had made a real mess of his hands. Maybe the imbalance in his adrenal gland did more than help him run fast?

The sound of police sirens drifted up from below. Zak leaned over the balcony. Three police vans were pulling up at the entrance to the building. But a black van had already arrived, and people were running towards the entrance.

Project 17 people.

"I'll see if I can find something to bandage your hands," said Dodge.

Limping a little, Zak followed his friend into the room. The dark-haired man was sprawled unconscious by the wall. Just beyond the arch, the pale-eyed man was also down, stretched out on his front with his hands tied behind his back with his own belt.

Zak gazed at Dodge as he crouched by the dark-haired man and started ripping strips from his shirt. Dodge had taken them both down in a matter of seconds.

"Dodge?" he asked, his voice subdued. "Who are you?"

Dodge glanced around at him. "The grave soul keeps its own secrets," he said, his voice sombre. "You know everything about me you need to know, Zachary. I'm your friend and I'm called Dodge. The rest is silence." His dark eyes bored into Zak. "I shan't ask you what these two men were doing up here with that peculiar piece of equipment – and you won't ask me about my past. Are you okay with that?"

Zak nodded.

It seemed that he would have to be.

Zak sat in a chair opposite Colonel Hunter's desk. His hands were bandaged, but the doctors had said the injuries weren't serious.

The Colonel was leaning forwards, his fingers steepled together.

"What does the man you call Dodge know about Project 17?" the Colonel asked.

Zak squirmed a little. "I told him some stuff about it a while back," he said, uneasy under Colonel Hunter's steely grey eyes. "He got involved in it during that whole business with Rina – I thought he ought to know the truth." He looked into the Colonel's eyes. "I trust him," he said. "I totally trust him. He'd never say anything."

"What did you tell him about Operation Firewall?" asked the Colonel in the same quiet, level voice.

"Not a thing," said Zak. "He followed me. I told him not to . . . but . . ."

"You say he told you he used to be a soldier?" said the Colonel.

Zak nodded.

"Do you know his real name?" the Colonel asked.

"No."

Colonel Hunter nodded and closed the folder that lay open on his desk. "I'll have to run some checks on him," he said. "But if he's clean, I see no reason why we need involve him further." One eyebrow rose quizzically. "Or disturb the unusual lifestyle he has chosen."

"Thanks," breathed Zak. He had been worried that Dodge's involvement in the operation might cause him some trouble.

"I know he means a lot to you, Quicksilver," the Colonel continued. "And I believe you when you say he can be trusted. But you put us all at risk every time you tell him something he doesn't need to know. Do you understand me?"

"Yes, Control," murmured Zak.

"Strictly, I should take preventative action to make sure there can't be any breach of security," said the Colonel. "But I'm sticking my neck out for you, Quick-silver. See that you deserve my trust." Colonel Hunter leaned back. "Dismissed," he said.

Zak hesitated. "What's going to happen now with Burning Sky?" he asked.

A gleam came into the Colonel's eyes. "Our top scientists are trying to reassemble the pieces of the device you threw off the balcony," he said. "But I'm not convinced it will do them any good. Bug has been through all the files on Dr Avon's laptop and there don't seem to be any details of how Burning Sky worked. I think the secrets of the EMP weapon will die with its inventor."

Zak got up and walked to the door. But another question was churning in his mind. A question he *had* to ask. He turned, his stomach turning over, his heart beating rapidly.

"Who is Jason Trent?" he asked.

The Colonel's eyes narrowed. "I see I shall have to have a stern word with Bug," he said in a low growl.

"It's not Bug's fault," said Zak. "I saw something by accident. An MI5 page. It said Slingshot's name was Jason Trent . . . but that he was also known as Jason Wyndham."

"That's correct," said the Colonel.

"He was my father, wasn't he?" Zak blurted in a rush. "You told me his name was John, but I think it was Jason – and he was an MI5 agent as well as my mother." Zak took a step forwards. "Please tell me the truth," he said. "I have to know the truth."

Colonel Hunter watched him thoughtfully for what seemed like a very long time. Zak found it impossible to guess what he was thinking. His eyes were like steel shutters, hiding a thousand secrets.

"Slingshot is not your father," Colonel Hunter said at

last, breaking a silence that had tightened around Zak's head like a steel band.

"Then who is he?" Zak shouted, unable to contain his emotions any more. "I want to know who he is!"

The Colonel opened a drawer in his desk and drew out a red folder. He looked at it for a few moments, his brow furrowed. Then he opened it and took out a brown envelope from among other typewritten papers. He took a photograph out of the envelope and slid it across the desk.

Puzzled, Zak walked back to the desk. The photo was a family snapshot. A man and a woman, and a boy Zak guessed must be about eight years old. The woman had a baby in her arms. They were all smiling. A curious tingling sensation burned in Zak's stomach as he looked at those happy faces.

"Who are they?" he asked, his voice thick in his throat.

"Your family," said the Colonel. His finger moved forwards and tapped the photo just above the boy's head. His words crashed into Zak's brain with all the force of a speeding bullet.

"This picture was taken ten days after you were born," the Colonel told him. "The boy is Jason Trent. He's your brother."

*

Zak sat cross-legged on a bed in Med. Sec. 1 of Fortress.

The room was full of other Project 17 agents, and everyone was in high spirits. Switch and Moon and Wildcat were sitting on the bed, laughing and joking. Operation Firewall was over except for the paperwork. Burning Sky was in about a thousand pieces, spread out on a workbench in one of Fortress's Sci Labs while a bunch of white coats tried to fit it all back together again.

"So, tell us again how that down-and-out mate of yours saved your neck," said Jackhammer, laughing. "That's my favourite part of the whole story!"

Zak rolled his eyes. "You've heard it three times," he said. "You're going to have to wait now till they green-light a movie about me."

"Codename Quicksilver – The Movie!" laughed Wildcat. "I can just see it!"

Zak laughed along with the others. There was still some pain in his arms and chest, but nothing that could mess with his good mood right then.

He hadn't told his colleagues about Colonel Hunter's revelation concerning Jason Trent. He needed to keep that to himself for a while. He wanted time to get his head around the astounding idea that he had an older brother.

The white coats had told him that they'd be running some special tests on him over the next few days. They wanted to learn more about his amazing feat of strength up on the balcony. Zak thought he already knew what had happened. He remembered something that he'd been told when he'd first been examined by Project 17 white coats.

You've only scratched the surface of what you're capable of...

Amazing speed, incredible strength? Things were getting interesting!

The folder on Operation Mozart was officially closed.

Alexi was back with his grandmother for a few weeks of rest and recuperation. The official line from his management was that he'd been taken ill – but that the American tour would be going ahead as previously scheduled after a brief delay.

A forensic FBI search of the villa Eldorado on Mad Cat Cay had revealed that everything belonging to Conquistador had been destroyed – including all notes, files and prototypes of the Burning Sky weapon. A single body had been found in the debris. Two more bodies had been located in the wrecked Range Rover in three metres of water at the bottom of the high cliff that linked the two halves of the island.

Pavlos Milos and the Russian called Boris were in police custody, charged with offences under the Counter-Terrorism Act. All the general public knew of the entire operation was that two men had been prevented from committing a barbaric attack on London. There was, of course, absolutely no mention of Project 17.

The door opened and a woman's head appeared.

"Quicksilver, when you have a moment, Dr Jackson would like to see you in his lab."

"Okay, I'm coming," said Zak, shuffling off the bed. Dr Jackson was one of Project 17's top scientists.

"I think those tests they threatened you with are about to get going," said Switch with a grin. "See you when they're through – if there's anything left of you by then."

Moon grabbed his wrist, her eyes shining. "We did good, Silver," she said. "Quite the team!"

He nodded, smiling as he headed for the door. He glanced around at his friends and colleagues. He remembered Dodge's words from earlier that morning.

Life's good today, Zachary. Very good.

Turn the page for a sneak
preview of Zak Archer's
next mission:
Killchase

CHAPTER **ONE**

TIME LEFT BEFORE DETONATATION:
00:01:23

Zak Archer was finding it difficult to hold the little torch steady between his teeth while he worked on the bomb. The room was in darkness, apart from the small wavering pool of white light, and he needed both hands free to very gently remove the last screw from the casing and lift the curved metal hatch in order to reveal the tangle of wires within.

He tried desperately to remember everything he

had been taught in Project 17's Explosive Ordnance Disposal classes.

This was one time when his special abilities were useless to him. Being able to run like the wind wasn't going to help him in this situation. What was needed here was focus and caution and pinpoint accuracy.

One careless moment, one jittery move, and it would all be over.

The bomb was packed inside a plastic box. Zak had already checked for booby-trap wires on the lid and for the telltale signs that the bomb was radio controlled. If the trigger was a mobile phone, the device could go off in his face at any moment.

His body prickled uncomfortably and his heart was pounding so loudly that it felt as if he had a drum under his ribcage. His hands shook and his head throbbed.

Cautiously, he removed the hatch from the casing and checked for sensors.

There was a trembler attached to the inside of the casing. If he'd tried to move the bomb, the trembler would have set it off.

His hair was hanging damp in his eyes and he had to keep blinking to clear his vision of stinging sweat.

He glanced at the digital countdown. 00:01:02.

If this were a movie, he'd be choosing between the

red and the green wires. Which to cut? *Red? No! Green?*
No ... wait ...

Except that all the wires in the bomb were yellow.

Using the tip of his tongue, Zak angled the torch beam to one side.

Gotcha!

He could see the battery pack in its TPU casing.

The heart and brain of the bomb.

He lifted a shaking hand and slid his fingers in through the yellow wires.

The trembler wire quivered.

Stop.

Breathe. Calm down. Forget the cramp growing in your legs. Forget the countdown.

His hand slid deeper into the device, brushing past the wires.

Large dark drops of sweat splashed onto the metal casing.

He stopped breathing. The blood surged through his head, making it hard to concentrate.

His fingertips reached the micro-plug in the battery.

He took it between the sides of his index and forefinger and gently eased it out.

It came loose and fell away.

The digital display stopped at 00:00:27.

Zak rocked back on his heels and let out a long whoop of breath.

Lights flickered on.

"Well done, Quicksilver."

It was Colonel Hunter's voice, coming over an intercom.

Zak spat the torch into his palm and stood up. His legs were still shaking, but all the worry and uncertainty had already drained away.

He gave a relieved smile as he gazed across the room to the mirror that almost filled one wall. In the reflection, he could see the various items of training and fitness equipment that surrounded him.

There was a room behind the mirror, and in that room he knew there were a group of people who had been watching him work on the bomb.

"How did I do?" he called.

"You'll get your official assessment in due course," came the Colonel's disembodied voice. "But you haven't finished just yet."

The door opened and Dr Jackson entered, followed by a few other white-coats. One of them scuttled over to the bomb, peered into it and scribbled some notes on a clipboard.

"Good morning, Quicksilver," said Dr Jackson, scrutinizing Zak from behind his thick horn-rimmed glasses.

He gestured across the room. "The treadmill, if you don't mind."

Zak didn't mind at all. Trying to defuse a dummy bomb in front of a whole lot of hidden observers had been nerve-wracking, but running a few kilometres on a treadmill would be fun. It would also help release the energy that he'd built up over the past few hours while he'd been reading and re-reading his bomb disposal notes.

A couple of the white-coats attached sticky monitor pads to Zak's chest, back and temples and fed thin wires into various electronic devices set up by the treadmill.

"We'll start easy, then see how it goes," said Dr Jackson as Zak climbed onto the treadmill.

"Fine with me." Zak glanced again at the long mirror. He didn't know exactly who was behind there, apart from Colonel Hunter, but he was aware that they were VIPs and he was determined to give them a good show.

Dr Jackson set the speed of the treadmill and the black conveyer belt began to move. Zak jogged along. The pace was way too easy. He was never going to burn off any energy at this rate. He looked around at Dr Jackson.

Dr Jackson nodded and increased the speed slightly. Zak ran along, putting his hands into his pockets and yawning. He saw one or two of the white-coats grinning.

"Are we starting the test soon?" Zak asked with a wry smile.

Dr Jackson pressed some buttons and the treadmill began to get faster.

"Subject is now running at ten kilometres an hour," Dr Jackson said, speaking to the watchers behind the window. "I have him on an incline of twelve per cent. His heart rate is at the level one would expect from this degree of exertion. All stress monitors are showing reactions that fall within usual parameters."

"Boring!" Zak said with a grin. "Crank it up a bit more, Doc, I'm falling asleep here!" He was really beginning to enjoy himself. "Kidding!" he added. He didn't want Hunter to think he was getting too cocky.

Dr Jackson punched a few more buttons. The belt was whipping away beneath Zak's feet now. His hands were out of his pockets, the lazy grin gone from his face as his arms pumped at his sides.

"Subject now running at twenty kilometres per hour," Dr Jackson said, his eyes on the treadmill's display screen. "Heart rate rising."

Zak ran, his eyes half-closed, concentrating straight ahead of him. He was close to his special place. He was nearly in the zone – that point where the gears in his head and body seemed to mesh and running became so effortless.

Zak was so focused on his running he was only vaguely aware of Dr Jackson's voice now. "This is where it starts to get interesting," Dr Jackson was saying. "Watch your monitors, ladies and gentlemen. You will see that the heart rate has settled to a lower level than previously, and you will also see how the imbalance in the subject's adrenal gland is showing as increased activity in the hypothalamus. But note also that the increase in adrenaline is not causing the normal rise in blood pressure, nor the expected vascular constriction."

Dr Jackson tapped the buttons again and the belt was really flying. Zak was in the zone, sprinting at full speed, breathing steadily. His legs were working like pistons, his arms swinging smoothly at his sides as he breathed calmly in and out. He felt tireless and elated. He felt as if he could carry on doing this for the rest of the day.

"Subject is running at forty kilometres per hour," said Dr Jackson. "And this is where things really begin to get strange."

Zak grinned.

Effortlessly in the zone.

*

On the other side of the long two-way mirror, a row of chairs faced into the large training room where Zak was being put through his paces. Clamped to the arm of each chair was a tablet computer displaying the data being produced by Dr Jackson's diagnostic devices.

"Dealing with the bomb proves the boy is capable of the intelligent and skilled application of learned techniques," said a severe-looking but attractive woman in her forties. She looked at Colonel Hunter. "But that's not what we're here for, is it?" She was Colonel Pearce, head of the MI5 department that worked out of Citadel, one of the four subterranean secret services bases that existed under London: Fortress, Rampart, Bastion and Citadel.

"Not entirely," replied Colonel Hunter. "I thought it would be useful for you to see that he's capable of using his brain, as well as being gifted in other ways."

"I can see what you mean," said an elderly man with white hair and a neat beard. Major Connolly, head of Rampart leaned forward, staring through the mirror. "He's a remarkable child."

Lt-Colonel McDermott, head of Bastion, was a short, stocky man with a face like a bulldog. "Do you have any more like him hidden away, Colonel?" he growled.

Colonel Hunter gave a quiet smile. "Quicksilver is a

one-off, as far as we know," he said. "Dr Jackson tells us his abilities come from a glandular imbalance. Normally, the amount of adrenaline his body releases would be dangerous, but somehow he absorbs it and uses it to his advantage. Dr Jackson says he's never seen anything like it before."

"I can believe that," said Isadora Reed, an American woman wearing a smart and expensive business suit. "He's quite the athlete." Her face was tanned and her voice had the sharp tone of someone used to being obeyed. "But does he have any other tricks up his sleeves, Peter?"

"Possibly," said the Colonel. "That's something Dr Jackson is trying to find out."

"For what length of time can the boy run at forty kilometres per hour?" asked Lt-Colonel McDermott.

"I don't believe he's been tested to his limit," said Colonel Hunter. "We're moving forwards carefully with him. The last thing we want to do is to burn him out or cause him some permanent injury."

"No," replied the American woman. "I can see how you'd want to preserve such a precious asset, Peter." She leaned back, crossing her legs, her eyes narrowing as she watched Zak running in the other room. "He's an extraordinary piece of equipment. Would you consider loaning him out? There are some tests we could do back in Washington that would certainly reveal his potential."

"Not at the moment," Mr Mallin, Personal Private Secretary to the Home Secretary broke in. He was the youngest man in the room, somewhere in his thirties, tall and pale and wearing a pinstriped suit. He gave Isadora Reed a thin smile. "We'd like to know a lot more about him before we'd allow the FBI to get their hands on him."

Isadora Reed laughed. "You can't blame a girl for trying, John," she said casually. She looked at Colonel Hunter. "The Project 17 report on Mission Burning Sky says he showed impressive strength at one point. But it was a little vague on the details. What happened, Peter?"

"The Burning Sky device had been fixed to a brick wall with six ten-millimetre coach bolts," Colonel Hunter explained. "A fully grown man would have needed a crowbar and a lot of muscle to get it loose. From his report, it seems that Quicksilver pulled it off the wall with his bare hands in about fifteen seconds."

"Impressive," said Colonel Pearce. "And have you replicated this feat of strength, to see if he can repeat it at will?"

"Not yet," said the Colonel. "Quicksilver cut his hands quite badly when he did it, and we've been waiting for his injuries to heal completely."

Isadora Reed tapped her nails on the arm of her chair, watching Zak closely. "You seem to have quite the super-agent here, Peter," she said quietly. "Are we going to see some tests of his strength today?"

"That's the plan," replied Colonel Hunter. He pressed a button on his computer. "Dr Jackson? Move it along, please." He nodded towards the treadmill, where Zak was still sprinting. "Watch closely," he said, leaning back. "This could be very interesting."

"Hey! I was enjoying that!" Zak said as Dr Jackson tapped out a command on the treadmill consol and the belt began to slow down. "I could have carried on all day."

"I think that's probably a good reason to stop," said Dr Jackson. "I'd like to test you on some other equipment now, Quicksilver."

"Fine," said Zak, jumping off the belt. "Whatever you say."

Zak's confidence had come a long way since Colonel Hunter had first suggested he might have the abilities to become a Project 17 agent. Several months and a whole lot of physical and academic training later, Zak was beginning to feel as if he could handle anything the Colonel threw at him. Okay, so he'd sweated over that bomb, but he'd defused it safely with almost half a minute to spare.

Dr Jackson led him over to one of the weight machines, a heavy-duty piece of equipment with a leather seat and a lot of tubular steel attachments. Zak's fellow agent, Jackhammer, spent a lot of time on this machine, pumping his muscles till you could almost have painted him green and called him The Hulk. Zak wasn't as muscular as Jackhammer, but he was looking forward to testing himself on this particular piece of equipment.

Ripping the Burning Sky device off the wall had been totally amazing. He still couldn't quite believe he'd done it. All that strength. Out of nowhere. If Colonel Hunter hadn't insisted he take time to recover, he'd already have given some of these machines a good work-out, just to prove to himself it hadn't been a one-off.

"This machine comes with two levels of pulleys, pec fly, leg extension and curl," Dr Jackson said, talking to the watchers again. "It's capable of working all the major muscle groups and includes a weight stack that can generate over fifty kilos of resistance in certain exercises." He looked at Zak. "We'll start you off easy," he said. "Don't try to go beyond your natural limits."

Zak climbed onto the seat. "What would you like me to do first?" he asked, settling down.

"I think we'll start with the upper body," said Dr Jackson as the other white-coats gathered around.

"Okay, ready or not, here I go." Zak reached up and grabbed the rubber handles that were suspended from the steel frame above his head.

The running thing came so naturally to him that it didn't seem all that special – but summoning super-strength at will, that would really be something to feel proud of. He hoped he could do it. He really didn't want to fail in front of Colonel Hunter and the others behind the mirror.

"Okay, Quicksilver, I think that will do for today," said Dr Jackson.

Zak had no idea how much time had passed. He felt as if he'd been on that machine for hours.

Super-strength? Super-loser, more like.

The work-out had been a total disaster.

Well, no, not a total disaster, but he could tell Dr Jackson was disappointed in his performance. As he'd come to the limit of his capabilities in each different exercise, he'd heard Dr Jackson say something like, "Thank you, Quicksilver, that was good for a boy of your age. Shall we move on...?"

In other words, he was doing fine, but there was nothing spectacular happening. No great surge of strength like he'd felt when he'd pulled the Burning Sky device off the wall. No rush of power. No moment when he felt that *thing* in his head that meant he was in the zone.

Colonel Hunter's voice came over the intercom. "Go and take a shower, Quicksilver," he said. "Report to my office in thirty minutes."

Exhausted and deflated, Zak wandered to the showers. He let the hot water beat into his face. He'd failed. The strength thing must have been a one-off fluke. He wasn't so very special after all.

He was just some freak who could run fast.

Big deal.